RACE CHANGER

*America Votes If All People
Should Become One Color*

Volume II

RICK HYMAN

COPYRIGHT

ISBN: 978-0-578-60360-5

Published by: Ronda Hyman

Edited by: Ronda Hyman

Original Cover Art (front and back)
 by Rick Hyman ©2019

Illustrations by Rick Hyman ©2019

Contact: rickhyman@racechanger.com

Website: racechanger.com

ACKNOWLEDGEMENTS

With love and appreciation, I acknowledge my wife, Ronda, for going on this Sci-Fi journey with me, and to all the people who read and loved Volume I, and to all the people who are looking forward to reading Volume II. Enjoy the Journey!

ABOUT THE AUTHOR

Rick Hyman was born and raised in N.E., Washington, DC. He attended The American University in Washington, D.C. and met his wife, Ronda on the campus there. After moving to California and living there for several years he received a Resolution Award at the California State Capitol for his art and writing, and a National Award for his project, "An Uncommon Journey to Diversity," held at the Milken Jewish Community Center with five Los Angeles city and valley schools. Hyman's historical family paintings traveled with the Virginia Museum of Fine Arts for 10 years. His art has been exhibited in many museums and art institutions around the country. Rick Hyman is the Author of Race Changer: First Encounter With Aliens, Volume I and co-Author of the book, *My Texas Family: An Uncommon Journey to Prosperity.*" He is also the Illustrator for a children's book, *"The Runaway Mango."*

CONTENTS

CONTENTS
(continued)

CHAPTER 1 Reba Travels to Mars

The Race Changers barely escape with their lives as they make their way back through the wormhole from 16th Century Rome to America on planet Earth. Their spacecraft is now cruising at a moderate and comfortable speed in an orbit miles above Earth. After dodging those ghost pirate ships in the Bermuda Triangle and that bad alien spacecraft that was on their tail trying to gain entry into their spacecraft, they were now in a state of rest and relief.

Zoey asks, "Can anyone tell me why we were battling ghost pirates?"

Solar Boy answers, "It's about good versus evil. Our Race Changer group is about good and Zardoff and his bad aliens are about evil. Remember his mission is to destroy the universe and mankind on Earth. He hates people of color and he will soon be here to look for them. If he sees them, he will wipe out people and the planet. That's why we must hurry and change the remaining Black, Indian, Spanish, Asian and all other races to White."

"What a racist!" says Zoey.

"Yes he is," said Solar Boy. "We have to destroy him in due time, so that we can change the people of color back to their original color like before."

Just for fun, Reba starts pushing buttons on the arm of her chair while everyone is relaxing.

"I am bored to death you guys. You know I'm always looking for some action," Reba says.

"If she's not looking for action, she's trying to steal some fine Diva's boyfriend," said Sharon.

"You hussy, shut up!" scoffed Reba.

Then Reba pushes another button on the arm of her chair and is suddenly ejected from the spaceship through an opened hatch. They all scream in shock over what just happened.

"Well, she said she was looking for some action," said Sharon.

Zoey yelled, "Reba, watch out for that wormhole passing by!"

The wormhole sucks Reba right into it with so many different colors glowing and she's spinning around and around, then she disappears.

"Where did she go?" cried Zoey."

"I let her have her adventure," said Solar Boy.

After a few minutes Reba's head pops up out of the ocean on some planet in a distant galaxy and she's pushed up onto the shore by the waves of the ocean.

"Where am I?" Reba utters out of breath, as she struggles to stand up. She looks around and sees a flat horizon with large planets in the sky. Now steady on her feet, she walks towards something or someone sitting on the shore. It's draped from head to toe in a light blue garment. "Where in the world am I and who are you?" She reaches out slowly to touch the cloaked being, but her hand goes right through it, even though she can still see the image of it. Reba is stunned. "I can't feel you—you must not be real. Is that you grandmother?"

The mysterious cloaked being said, "Yes, it is me, Reba. I am always here for you even if you are in another time period in a far-off galaxy."

"Am I dreaming," asked Reba?

"No, my child, you are on Mars."

"Wow!" shouts Reba excitedly.

"Grandmother, I see pyramids over there, like the ones in Egypt. I want to touch them."

"You are in the future, Reba. You must be careful because if you go into those pyramids without knowing certain secrets, you might not return."

Reba, mesmerized, begins to walk into an oasis or jungle. "OMG!" yells Reba. She sees huge dinosaurs with their long necks walking past the pyramids and castles made out of colorful crystals in the distance. Then she hears footsteps, so she hides and thinks, *I must get closer to the pyramids and that beautiful, magnificent structure. The pyramids are calling me.* After walking about a mile towards them, she begins to feel sand under her feet and senses that something is not right. Then she hears clank, clank, clank. It's the sound of metal and motors. She then runs and jumps under a big bush. The noise gets louder and louder. She peeps out from under the bushes and sees giant metal robots marching like an Army, hundreds of them. They look futuristic. A spaceship appears floating above Reba. She looks up and says, "Oh shit!" Then a door opens and a laser beam shines down out of the alien spaceship on her. As the giant metal robot army march pass her, one robot turns his head and looks Reba into her eyes and winked as though he knew her. Then it flies up into the air close to the spaceship. It raises its arm and shoots a powerful blue and white light of electricity at the spaceship. Then it catches fire, drops to the ground and burns on the sand 50 yards from Reba.

After the army of robots pass her, she decides to make a run for the pyramids. She looks up in the air and sees something silver and round just hanging in the sky, very still. It's too small to be the moon. "Is it a planet or a satellite," she asks herself. She continues to walk towards the pyramids. It must be about 12 of them. Then she sees several spacecraft flying in front and over them. It appears to be some kind of town made up entirely of crystal castles.

Oh my God! I never new there were pyramids and castles on Mars. Am I in the past, present, or future? Grandmother said I was in the future, but which dimension? She then calls out, "Grandmother, help me, help me!"

Her grandmother speaks and says, "Reba, you will find many mysteries if you continue this Mars journey. Turn back Reba. You must return to Earth and work with that noble space traveler Solar Boy. You will marry him one day. You two will save Earth, the Universe, and mankind as you know it. You can now go forward into the pyramids to find the key to unlock the clear path to exit this planet safely. Your Prince is awaiting your return to Earth. You are needed. The invasion of Zardoff is imminent, so you must go back."

Thoughts run through Reba's mind, *I just want to get close enough to the pyramids to touch the outside walls. I have to see if it's real or an illusion. I have never seen anything like this. I hope the Race Changer group can see this one day.*

Spacecraft are flying by every few minutes now, faster and faster. In the distance, Reba can hear fighting and battling between the spacecraft above, and the robots below. *I might have a few minutes to touch the walls of the pyramids and then run back to the beach and get the hell out of here.* "Okay, its clear now, run girl, run!" she shouts out loud.

It's hot and there is a sand storm that suddenly kicks up and is headed right towards her. She opens up her backpack and pulls out her space suit that Solar Boy gave her and quickly puts it on—just in time. Now the sand is blowing and swirling in the wind, approaching her at about 600 miles an hour. She can barely see. The wind picks her up off the ground and into the air for a few seconds and then drops her 20 yards from the pyramids. She runs towards them but falls into a huge crater. She tries to grab onto the walls of the crater as she slides downward. Unable to get a grip and hysterical, she thinks to herself, *Oh no, I can't stop sliding down. There's some kind of force pulling me into it.* Lots of dirt is falling on her and out of nowhere comes a huge brontosaurus dinosaur upside down falling on the left side of her. Then she sees another dinosaur also falling upside down

17

with its legs up in the air, screaming on the right side of her. It just barely misses crashing into her. "Dammit," she says. Dirt from above and everything else is being sucked into this crater. *If I hit the bottom, I will surely die.* Right then, a small ledge sticking out from the side of the crater catches her fall. She's breathing hard from fright and shock, and adrenalin is rushing through her body. She watches as more robots, and spacecraft pass her spiraling out of control towards the bottom. She looks to her left and sees a narrow pathway leading into a cave. She stands up and is able to walk and follow the path. She reaches an open space that looks like a parking garage with several futuristic spacecraft parked in it. Reba notices that one of them is just big enough for one, maybe two people. She is so nervous. She smooths her hair back and wipes sweat from her brow, not knowing what she will find next.

She notices another door inside this unusual alien parking garage, but this one has a glowing light around it.

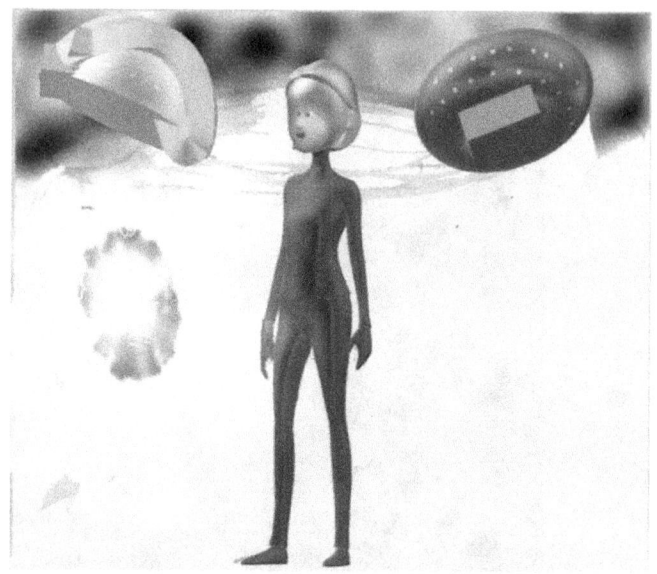

She goes over and opens it and sees a wormhole spinning vertically. It's dark inside of it but very colorful outside and all around it. It's giving off a humming noise. She says aloud, "I don't know if I'm ready for this. If I go into this wormhole it could take me somewhere else in the universe

billions of light years from Earth."
Remembering the warnings of her
grandmother she thinks—*Nope! I don't
think so.* She then backs up and closes the
door.

She walks over to that cute little
spacecraft and needing to hear a human
voice, she says out loud, "Ah ha! I get it.
This belongs to some space traveler who
leaves their vehicle parked here until they
return from their journey back through that
wormhole. Then they come through that
door over there and jump into their
spacecraft and go flying around Mars. Well,
I'm going to take this spacecraft and hope I
can figure out how to fly it out of here!" So
she steps inside the small craft and sits
down. She can hear the soft loving voice of
her grandmother. 'Think what you want to
happen, and it will happen.' Then Reba

pushes a button and closes her eyes, and she can see the spacecraft flying in her mind.

Magically, the ceiling opens up and the craft becomes airborne and flies up and out of the crater. She can now see the orange-red surface of Mars. As she flies, she can see the ocean and beach and lots of multi-colored plant life. She's high above the castles and pyramids. She looks down and sees military type robots, and Martian people. They are florescent lime green, 10 feet tall, and very skinny. They have colonized this part of Mars, working and living there. Then some other larger spaceships appear and are flying next to her.

Reba thinks, *Oh, I hope they don't shoot me down. I wish me and my spaceship were invisible.* And just like that, she and

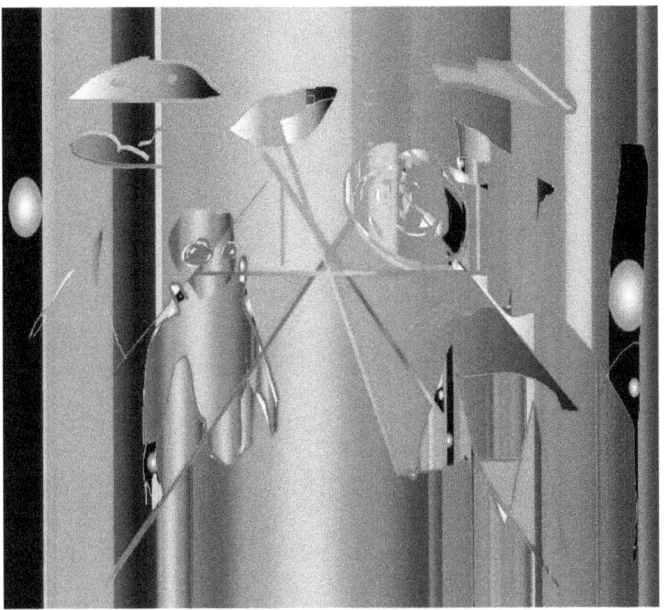

her spacecraft disappear and the unknown spaceships stop looking for her and flew away from her. Then Reba and her spaceship lands on the beach where she arrived when she was washed up onto the shore. She gets out of the spacecraft, takes off her spacesuit and yells, "Mars, I will return."

So Reba runs back into the water and is hurled up, down and around in the swirling waves and strong winds, and is back into present day time. She comes barreling back through the same hatch she was thrown out of on the spaceship. Zoey jumps out of her seat and rushes over to her. She is on the floor coughing and almost choking, and is soaking wet. She hugs Reba tightly and asks her, "Girl, where did you go and are you okay?" All the other Race Changers, now relieved, go over and hug Reba too.

Rion says, "I knew you would get her back here safely Solar Boy."

"Thanks Rion, that little rendezvous was quite a cure for her boredom, but she's a real warrior, I admire her." says Solar Boy.

"I went to Mars. I will tell you about it later. I need to rest now," said Reba, yawning.

Solar Boy smiles while watching Zoey console her sister.

"I think we should go to NASA in Florida before we go to see the President. That way, NASA can be our escorts and give us clearance when we go to Washington, DC," said Rion.

"And, they will see that Solar Boy and I are not a threat," said Space Girl. "We can work together on coming up with a plan to defeat Zardoff, the Alien leader. Finally, they will hear directly from us about what is really going on and realize that we are allies."

At NASA's Kennedy Space Center, everyone is rushing around preparing for the Race Changers' arrival. The Press is out in large numbers, the Governor and other dignitaries.

"Be ready to shoot them with tranquilizer guns should they become hostile. Do we have an ETA?" said one of the Special Agents.

"All we know is that they will arrive tonight. Our radar is unable to pick up their spacecraft," answered another agent.

On Solar Boy's spaceship, the Race Changers are excited about their meeting with NASA. Reba says, "I just really love helping our country and planet Earth. I have always dreamed of this."

Sharon is combing through her long blond hair. "They'll take one look at us kids and think we're a joke, trying to pretend to be astronauts or something."

"Yeah," Ava said. "We might have to use our Race Changing guns on them to show'em we mean business." They all laugh.

"Now girls," said Sabrina, "Don't get too ahead of yourselves. No one is going on an ego trip here. Our focus is not about power, it's about saving lives. We only use power to save lives, not jeopardize our mission."

"I know Miss Sabrina," said Ava, but it just feels so good to carry a weapon. I mean, I used to be all timid and shy, but since we've been on this mission and had to kill those vamps and zombies, I feel like a new person. I mean, I've really grown up. Please don't take this the wrong way, but I like kicking ass. I feel so empowered."

Rion walks over to the girls and says, "Okay, enough chit-chatting about power, weapons and kicking ass." No one knows how they will feel until they are faced with a situation and put to the test. You guys are so innocent, but on the other hand, you stepped up to the plate when faced with life and death situations. I'm very proud of you, but at the moment you're missing some of your childhood. However, our planet and it's people are worth it. And you'll always have this mission to look back on with pride."

"That is, if we win this insane war with Zardoff and his disgusting crew," said Sabrina.

Reba is just waking up from her nap after her excursion from being ejected into the wrath and fury of raging water, wormholes and Mars.

"How much longer before we are arrive at NASA?" asked Reba.

"Perfect timing, Reba," answered Solar Boy. "Prepare for landing at the Kennedy Space Center."

CHAPTER 2 Changing Into a White Man

The Race Changers are in a meeting with two NASA Scientists and two CIA Agents.

"Gentlemen, we have two young Black men here who have volunteered to participate in this exercise with your Race Changing machine," said CIA Agent #1. "They have been briefed and are ready."

The two Black men, one tall and the other short enter the room. They both look about 25 years of age. Scientist #1 says, "Okay, we are ready whenever you are."

Solar boy shoots them with his Race Changing machine gun. In a matter of seconds, the two Black men are changed into White men and have White features. They stare at each other and look in a mirror at themselves, flabbergasted.

The scientists and agents in the room are in awe. "Oh my gosh! I don't believe this," says Scientist #2.

The tall, newly changed White man says, "Hey, I'm White, what do I do now? I don't know how to act like a White man. Where do I learn how to act White? Am I a hybrid or a robot, what the hell am I? If you guys are experimenting on my body, then I want a retirement pension for me as a Black man and another pension for me as a White man. I also want to be put on your payroll and get paid every week. Oh! I want my family to get insurance benefits if something happens to me."

"Now calm down," said CIA Agent #1. "We will get you to personnel and they will take care of all that in a minute."

Scientist #1 whispers to Scientist #2, "I don't know if he's acting like a hood guy or a White guy. He sounds like he's gone haywire."

Scientist #2 replies, "To me, he's acting like some big CEO mogul in the Board Room trying to close some million dollar deal."

"Yes, of course! I agree," said Scientist #1.

Scientist #2 says to the tall, newly changed White male, "Your name is now Brady." Then he looks at the short, newly changed White male and says, "And your name is David."

They both jump for joy and high five each other.

"I can't wait to go into a boardroom at fundraiser meetings and cocktail parties!" says David.

Brady asks the NASA scientists, "Is there a school we can go to where somebody can teach us how to be White?"

"Yeah," says David, "how do you act White?" And if we ever have babies, will they come out looking White or Black?"

NASA Scientist #1 said, "I don't know. We are just learning about this machine."

"You know guys, just act like you see them act on TV. Know all about sports, money, drive your antique car on the weekends…get it?" said Scientist #2.

Reba whispers to Solar Boy, "Wow, such interesting questions. I never knew that there was so much to this race thing."

"Well Reba, there are some very important elements that are the same in all outer solar systems, like Peace, Love, Hate,

Energy, Time, Light, Darkness, and Race," says Solar Boy.

Reba goes to the bathroom and as she walks down the hallway, she passes a lab and overhears a real sneaky looking Scientist talking on his cell phone.

The Scientist says, "Okay Butler, thanks for telling me they were coming. I'm getting lots of secrets about the universe from Solar Boy. Me and one of my energy scientists know just what to do with the information. We will send a check to your PO Box, and don't worry, we won't tell your boss, Mr. Diamond. If you get a chance, you can tell Zardorff that in the future we will soon be making robots and hybrids with an evil hate chip implanted in them so that he can conquer Earth and the Universe.

Reba almost staggers to the bathroom in shock. She throws some cold water on her face and stares at herself in the mirror, wondering what to do next. Then she dials a number on her cell phone. *I hope I can reach the Rabbi at the Temple*, she thought.

The Rabbi answers. Reba tells him what is going on. The Rabbi says, *Let me see if I have this right, Reba. Evil robots conquering the universe with evil/hate microchips in them.* He tells her to be calm and to just play the role and act normal, and to get out of there alive, and to tell Rion and Solar Boy what she heard as soon as she gets the chance. "Reba, here at the Temple, we will take up a donation for you Race Changers because you are doing God's work and we support you. Keep going, my child." Then he hangs up.

Reba smooths down her dark reddish hair and puts on some lipstick that she had in her pocket. After composing herself, she goes back into the laboratory and joins the others.

Newly White man David asks, "When I die, will I get into heaven? What church do I go to now?"

Brady ignores David's question and says, "I guess I want to learn about stocks so I can be in the Wall Street Journal and play the stock market and make millions."

David says, "I can't wait to walk down the street in the hood!" I know it's going to be a powerful feeling."

Then Brady says, "You might be putting your life at risk if you go down the wrong street—I mean, being White and all."

"Yeah, but I know the streets, and I can handle myself."

"Okay, but don't forget who you are now, so act the part. You're a White man, and if you walk down certain streets acting like some mogul you might get mugged by some bad guys who don't want you there."

NASA Scientist #1 says, "When we get ready to do some research or experiment in the hood, we'll call you guys, but for now go and live your life."

Brady asks the Scientists and NASA Agents, "Well, since you all are White, what do you do on the weekends? Or should I say, what do 'we' do on weekends?"

Scientist #2 responds, "I play golf and I wash my dog. I drive my vintage 1946 Ford Sportsman Deluxe to the market. I play fantasy football and watch it on TV."

Brady says, "I bet you are counting your money, and I mean millions in the bank everyday too." Brady laughs, "You didn't tell us that, huh?"

"Well, I don't know if everybody White is doing that," responds Scientist #2.

"Yeah," says Reba, "I'm sure there are some Black people that are doing that too. Millionaires, no matter what race they are have to watch their money. That's what I learned in my Economics class."

"We will follow you wherever you go, and we will send a drone to fly over and protect you," said Scientist #1.

"What?" says Brady, "A drone to protect me? What the hell is a drone going to do for me except let you and Big Brother, or as they said back in the day, 'the Man,' spy on me and my friends in the hood and see what we are about to steal next. No, sorry, I didn't mean steal, but you know what I mean, man."

"Yeah," said David, "Like they say, 'the man,' or Big Brother is everywhere and he knows everything. He can see you but you can't see him. They need to change that name too cause he ain't big and he don't look like a brother. They need to call 'the Man,' Big Sneaky! Cause he's slithering around like a damn snake getting information on people for no good reason."

They all laugh.

Brady says, "That frickin' drone don't know what I know. I will lose that sucker in the first 24 hours, watch."

NASA tells them that they will now begin to work with other governments in all the countries to change every race to the White race, because the bad aliens are coming on January 1, New Year's Day.

"How will we know the bad aliens are here, and will we know what they look like?" asked Reba.

NASA Scientist #2 responds, "Well trust me, you will know. Our sources tell us that they are the ugliest things in the Universe. They have millions of flying ships that will fill every inch and a mile high in the sky above."

Brady and David's jaws drop and they look at each other and then at the NASA Scientists.

David says, "Hey, we need a drink after hearing this, come on you NASA big shots, I know you got some powerful biotechnical new drug you have been experimenting with and probably using it to enjoy yourselves that the public don't know about. Let us in on the secret."

Scientist #2 says, "We have top secrets that are not up for discussion here."

"Come on man, we are all the same race now and you probably even have some sexy female aliens or sexy women robots that will blow our minds hiding in the closet in your home or office, right?"

CIA Agent #1 says, "Okay, guys. We know that becoming White is going to take some getting used to. Just know that we are here to help you however we can, but soon you won't be alone, because once everyone is changed to White, it will get easier and seem more natural."

David says, "Just give me some fat pockets cause I'm one of the first to become White and I want to be paid the big bucks. I gots to take care of my Mom and sisters and brothers. We gotta get something out of this crazy shit. What if I die of an incurable White disease that Black folks don't get?

Then that is it for my Black ass, oh…my bad, I mean my Black-White ass."

"Hey, have you mad scientists changed any Black females to White yet?" asked Brady.

Scientist #1 answered, "No."

David says, "I'm going to have to call my lawyer and sue NASA for gender discrimination."

"What?" responded Scientist #1. "Now wait a darn minute, I have been working here for 30 years and I am not going to let some Black-White man Frankenstein experiment jeopardize my retirement plan with some silly lawsuit."

Agent #1 says, "If you'll excuse me,

I'm going to make a phone call."

Brady and David talk with the Race Changers. The girls touch and rub their arms to see if their White skin will come off. It doesn't. David flirts with Sharon and touches her blond hair. Rion and Sabrina take it all in, and laugh at the kids playing around with each other.

Agent #1 comes back into the room and says to Brady and David, "You know you guys are pretty smart, now that you're White."

Rion frowns in disgust at what the Agent said.

Agent #1 continues. "Our lawyers said that we have to see if the Race Changing machine works on Black females too."

Scientist #1 said, "Where can we find some Black women that would be willing to change their race from Black to White? Do we go to Watts or Harlem?"

Rion says, "Have you been asleep for the last 20 years Rip van Winkle? Most of Harlem is White now because of gentrification. You know—Whites moving in, Blacks pushed out."

David said, "You can look in South Central, LA. I'd like to see you White dudes looking for some Black female specimens there to take back to your lab. Hell, you'll be clocked within five minutes."

"Oh, Okay" said Scientist #1. "But let me remind you two that you are now White men, so act like it, you are not down in South Central on the corner with the homeboys. You must learn to speak proper English—the King's English."

David responds, "What do you know about South Central other than the 'Straight Outta Compton' movie was filmed there? You know you mad scientists with your studious look better not walk the streets in the hood or like I said, you'll be dead meat in no time. All I need to do is make one phone call."

Brady says, "You keep forgetting that you're a White man now."

"I know, I know." said David.

"Why don't we have a contest like when they audition actresses for TV or parts for a movie?" Brady asked.

Scientist #1 says, "See – now that's thinking like a White man. Good idea."

Reba says, "So you want to change some "sisters" into White girls? Good luck with that."

The Race Changers start laughing.

"Reba, the correct term is 'Sistas,' not 'Sisters,' said Sabrina.

Rion says, "Wow Reba, I didn't think you'd know to even call them "sisters."

"Mr. Rion, I know a lot more than you think I do," responded Reba with a smug look on her face. "I've been studying the Ebonics dialect."

The Scientists start laughing.

Then Sabrina jumps up and shouts, "Wait a damn minute! Are you Scientists making fun of our race? Rion, get them."

Rion gets up and walks towards the Scientists with a clinched fist.

Scientist #1 jumps up and nervously says, "Oh no, no, no, no, no Sabrina. This is just the government and NASA's experiment to save mankind."

With doubt and suspicion in her voice, Sabrina says, "Yeah right, just like when they said that some monkey jumped out of a tree in Africa and bit a man, and that's how Aids got started. It's all bull shit! Here we go again with the hoodwink on the backs of Black people. Reba is right, good luck with that. Just go ahead and get your experiment done so that we can move on."

Solar Boy says, "We have lots to do and not much time."

"Yeah, and I want NASA to pay me a consulting fee and I want to be on NASA's payroll for life and my grandkids for life too," said Brady.

Reba whispers to Zoey, "He's learning to be White real fast, he sounds like a real business man."

"Okay," says Scientist #2, rubbing his head. "Let's not get too carried away now. We can work all of this out with Human Resources later. Just remember, you two new White guys are the first ones whose race has been changed by the government of the United States so you have made history. Be careful for the rest of your life, cause everyone wants this secret."

Scientist #1 says, "I just had Zoey help me post an advertisement on Instagram to find some Black females from Los Angeles to participate in a scientific experiment with the government and get paid for it. I didn't mention the race changing part. They'll find that out after they respond to the ad."

"Good, good!" said Scientist #2.

"I want to be in the room watching when this happens," Rion said with a big smile on his face. "You White guys don't understand, you'd have to be Black to get it."

CHAPTER 3 Changing Into a
White Woman

A few days later, all of the same people including the two new White guys are back in the laboratory at NASA when three Black females arrive. Shelly is from Alabasas, California. She has expensive sunglasses on and is wearing a designer dress. She gets out of a limo with a Gucci purse on her arm. Lakeesha is wearing sweats and has sneakers on. Her mother and sister are with her. They are from South Central LA. She looks very angry. She is resisting and yelling. Her mother and sister are almost dragging her in. She's kicking and screaming. Big Baby is a short, dark skinned woman and weighs about 200 pounds. She's from Watts in LA.

"Come on honey," says the mother of

Lakeesha, "You know we all can spilt the money they're gonna pay us for you doing this."

"I don't wanna be nobody's guinea pig, I told you over and over again Mama," responds Lakeesha.

"I told you that after you are changed to White…."

The daughter interrupts and says, "Don't change me, don't change me." Her voice echoes throughout the corridors of NASA as they drag her down to the lab. "My mother just wants the lab money to buy more drugs."

"Shut the hell up child!" says her mother who sees the NASA agents standing nearby with their arms folded, looking mean. She asks, "Now where do you want us to put her, up there on this here table?"

NASA agent #1 says, "Not just yet, Mam."

"Change her ass quick! And while you're at it, can you get the meanness out too? She's always beatin' up on people. All she thinks about is going out with some man. I had to nail the window in her room shut cause she keeps sneaking out the house while I'm sleep. And she can't listen to nobody. She won't go to church, she won't work a job like normal people. All she wants to do is talk on the phone, use my car and go out with all them guys to the clubs all the time."

Lakeesha continues to wrestle with her mother and sister. A switch blade knife falls out of her pocket, and everyone jumps back. Their eyes get big with fear in them. They continue to wrestle, and then a 9 millimeter pistol falls out from under her clothes and hits the floor. The gun goes off. Everyone in the room ducks for cover as the bullets go ping, pong, ping, ricocheting off the floor, the walls, and the metal lab equipment. At least 12 rounds go off. After the room becomes silent, they all stand up and come out from where they were hiding. Lakeesha picks up her pistol and shoves it back into the waist of her sweat pants.

Seconds later, a huge wall rolls back and reveals what appears to be a humongous outdoor parking lot with hundreds, maybe even thousands of flying saucer shaped spacecraft lined up in rows. A few rows back of the spacecraft is what appears to be a man in a spacesuit with a helmet on, holding some type of laser gun. It's as if he's guarding the spacecraft. Everyone is completely shocked, especially not knowing what was going to happen next.

"What on Earth is that?" asks Reba. "I don't believe what I am seeing."

Lakeesha's mother says, "Ah shit child, you done gone too far this time. This bitch could never shoot straight anyway. Now here she is, done got us involved in some outta space shit."

"You can't ever say it right Mama. It's "outer" space—she spells it—O-U-T-E-R, not outta."

"We's all in trouble now girl, and don't you be correctin' me. You ain't no English teacher."

Scientist #2 says, "Well folks, you weren't supposed to know about this."

Then they hear a loud animal growling sound.

"What was that?" asked Zoey.

Everyone in the room takes two or three steps back.

Rion yells, "Grab your rifles and be ready to shoot! Sounds like something out of this world."

They look further down into that parking lot and see a 20 foot tall image of a man, also in a spacesuit that is glowing. He's growling and running towards the other man as if he's going to attack him.

"No, no!" says Reba. "He's not even turning around. He's going to get it! I can't look, he's about to be crushed."

Scientist #2 says, "Don't worry, you are looking at Virtual Reality. This is not really happening. We call it VR."

"I don't believe you," says Reba.

The 20 foot tall alien is now in clear view. He takes off his space helmet. His head looks like a big gray block that's been crushed, scrapped, and pulverized a thousand times. He's hideous looking. He grabs the other spaceman who was guarding the spacecraft and picks him up.

"Stop! No!" shouts Reba.

"Turn your head girls!" says Sabrina, "Don't look...you don't want to see what is about to happen."

The tall creature begins to eat the other spaceman like he was a piece of chicken or something. He pulls his arm off and gobbles it up. Then he pulls off his legs and gobbles that down too with blood dripping. Next, he bites off his helmet. His octagon shaped blue head rolls out of the helmet and onto the floor. It almost looks like a human head except for the shape of it, and it has four eyes, two in front and two in back. It rolls like a bowling ball towards the entrance of the laboratory where the Race Changers and Scientists are.

"Its coming this way, the head is rolling this way—look out!" yells Reba.

The eyeballs pop out but are still connected to its head by some type of coil or wire. They are bouncing up and down on the ground like a slinky.

"I can't take this."

Rion starts to laugh.

"Wait! Wait!" yells Reba.

The giant 20 foot alien is chasing that rolling head and now they are both coming towards the Race Changers.

Rion laughs even louder now.

"What the hell are you laughing at Rion?" asked Sabrina. "This is some scary shit!"

Then Rion says, "I can laugh cause its funny."

Now the others begin to laugh too, except Reba.

Zoey sits down in a lab chair and pulls out two cupcakes, and bites into one of them while watching the crazy virtual reality scene.

"This is not a movie!" shouts Reba.

The huge alien is still chasing the bloody rolling head with his mouth drooling as if the head will be the juiciest part of the meal. The spaceman's body that is without a head is chasing them both – his arms flinging wildly.

"What the hell is happening here?" asks Lakeesha. "Where are we? This is more action than on a Saturday night in Watts."

Scientists #2 says, "Like I said, this is just an experiment with virtual reality, its not really happening."

Out of nowhere they hear a big boom coming from the wall behind them and they turn their attention to the noise. The rolling head shoots through the wall into the room like it was shot out of a canon. Then comes the huge alien crashing through the same wall, and then the headless spaceman runs into the room through another door and grabs Reba.

"Here we go," says Rion, "Race Changers to the rescue."

Lakeesha pulls out her 9 millimeter, puts in another clip and reloads. She shoots the huge alien. Rion grabs his laser rifle off his back and blasts the headless spaceman. Both he and Reba fall to the ground. Then over the loud speaker they hear a voice that sounds very evil as if it were growling. It says, "This is Zardoff. I am not finished yet." The head that was shot back into the room then explodes, and now fire and smoke are coming from it.

"How dare him grab my girl," says Carlos. I was going to punch him. Hey, look over there. Looks like something is moving out of that cloud of smoke." They all turn and see six small zombie pit bulls angry and growling.

"Quick, quick, enough of this experiment!" shouts Reba.

"Shut it off!" yells Rion. He grabs Scientist #2 and shakes him roughly.

"Alright, alright," says Scientist #2. He goes over to the wall and pulls a lever and then the alien pit bulls disappear.

Lakeesha says, "Sorry guys, I'm from a tough neighborhood and it's a crazy world out there, so I have to protect my beautiful self. I might wear sweats a lot, but I know I am fine. You should see me when I hit the clubs. I can make a grown man cry just by watching me twerk."

Zoey starts laughing.

Lakeesha says to Zoey, "What are you laughing at?"

Reba jumps up and says, "My sister can laugh at whatever she wants to laugh at."

Scientist #1 presses the button on the phone's intercom and asks for Security to come to the Lab.

The White male lab technician is holding a Race Changing machine given to him by Solar Boy. He asks Lakeesha if she has any questions before he changes her into a White woman.

"Yeah," says Lakeesha, pointing to her face. She makes a circular motion around her face with her right hand open. "You see this beautiful, gorgeous face—see it? You can change this to White but from my waist down it's gold and the middle valley between my thighs is trimmed in platinum. The men love me, Baby."

"What is she talking about?" asked Reba."

Big Baby says, "She means don't change that part of her cause that part is precious."

"I am confused," said the White lab tech, "What is she talking about?"

The Scientists look at each other with puzzled looks on their faces.

Big Baby blurts out, "It means she's got some good boo-tay, you idiots!"

"Don't change me to White below my waist – keep all this sweet Blackness like the African Queen that I am," says Lakeesha.

Sabrina bursts into laughter.

Lakeesha continues, "That's right, every guy I make out with asks me to marry them. But before I go on a date with them I tell them that the last seven men I have been out with, and made out with, have asked me to marry them and that they are going to be number eight. They don't believe me at first. But before the night is over they are on their knees begging for my hand in marriage, saying they can't live without me."

Brady says, "Damn baby, I used to be Black, but now I'm White. Uh, after you get changed to a White woman, let's go on a date and get some dinner."

"What I got is too much for you little boy. I'm a big girl and my nickname is Miss Good Thighs."

Scientists #2 interrupts their conversation and says, "Okay technicians, move her up here and have her stand in this circle, then step back. I'm ready to change her to White."

Shelly from Alabasas asks Lakeesha,

"Why don't you want to be changed to White? I didn't know this experiment was about changing our skin color. I thought they were doing some kind of study on skin color. Oh hell no, forget this shit." She then hauls off and slaps Scientist #2, and his eyeglasses fall to the floor. He staggers and almost falls down but catches himself.

"Damn, she hit me!" Everybody laughs, especially Brady and David.

Shelly says to Brady, "What are you laughing at you fake White man. I'll slap you too."

Brady says, "Girl, you don't know who you are talking to. They just changed me from Black to White so this is just a disguise. I am still Big Slim the pimp inside. I will spend one night with you and you will go home to your husband with no panties on walking bow-legged with a permanent smile on your face, and then you'll kick his ass out the house after you ask for a divorce. Y'all don't know me."

"No you won't, fool. My husband is a famous music producer. We live in Alabasas, and I am a professional singer. I am here just for the shopping money. I ain't going to be changed from my pretty Black Diva self to a White woman. Let me out of here, but pay me first, please." She starts walking towards the door, but two lab assistants grab her by each arm. She tries to break free of them but they hold her firmly and walk her back to the middle of the room.

Big Baby, the girl from Watts says, "Now look, I don't want no shit from y'all impostors pretending to be Scientists. Before you change me to White, I need you to knock 80 pounds off me. Then I need my nails did and my hair dyed. Make it blond and shrink my lips some cause they're a little too big. And get rid of some of this ass of mine, but keep my boobs the same, cause the fellas like that."

Rion jumps up and says, "Why don't you guys just build a robot instead."

"Shut up you," said Big Baby.

"You got a lot of demands, Miss," says Rion. That ass thing is gonna happen anyway cause you know White women sometimes don't have big butts."

Lakeesha balls up her fists and yells, "Naw, forget it, y'all ain't gonna change me to White after you made my people work in the fields back in the day. This here is some type of sick experiment on Black people. I don't even believe no damn aliens are coming to destroy Earth either, like they say on the news."

Then she begins to punch and kick over tables in the lab and runs towards the door. The security guards grab her and one of the lab techs sedate her with an injection. She passes out and they pick her up and carry her to the examining table.

Reba asks, "Why is it that all of these Black girls have attitudes like they are so angry?"

"Good question," says Rion. "Its funny that the Black guys had no problem wanting to be turned to White, they were eager to be changed for better opportunities in life because of their White skin color."

"True," says Ava.

Rion continues, "Well everybody is different, but when people have been at the bottom of the economic ladder for so long, they will do almost anything to get ahead. A lot of Blacks will see this as an opportunity to come up in this country."

Scientist #2 jumps up and shouts, "Eureka! All three of these Black girls are perfect specimens to have their color changed."

"Specimens! Who the hell are you calling a specimen?" asks Big Baby. Your ass is a poor specimen of a man!"

"Okay, enough!" shouts Rion.

Scientist #2 whispers to Scientist #1. "This is going to be a good experiment. All of these Black women have that attitude like most Blacks. I wonder if they will have it when they are changed to White women, and will they prefer to date Black guys or White guys?"

A Lab tech leads the Black girls over to a platform and tells them to step up on it. Hesitating, they follow the tech's instruction. They look at each other as if it was for the last time.

Solar Boy walks over to the platform and shoots all three of them with his Race Changing machine. Everyone in the room utter sounds of 'Oh, ooh, wow.'

Shelly, the vain Producer's wife, steps
off the platform singing a country western
song.

She has blond hair and blue eyes now.
"Where is my agent? We are going to move
to Nashville," she says. "No more Alabasas
for us. I'm tired of all those Black
millionaire rappers moving next door and

having parties all night. They are taking over the neighborhood with their parties blocking my driveway. Me and my husband are moving out. Oh wait, wait, you have to change him too because he's my Producer and he's Black. He must be White like me. I will never get a record deal in the country music industry with him being Black. Anyway, somebody, please order me some catfish cause this country girl is starving.

Big Baby steps off the platform with sandy hair and a full figure of breasts, hips, ass and all—very curvy but not too big. She is much smaller than she was before. She looks at herself in the full length mirror and says, "Yep, its all there, now when I get out of here, I can get any man I want. I'm going to find me a rich Jew boy. That's what I will do, one that will take care of me cause I'm the whole package. Look at my fine, White self!" She turns around slowly and looks at all sides of herself. "He's got to build me a five million dollar house and buy me a Bugatti."

Lakeesha, the Tomboy by day and Sex Pot by night, steps off the platform and says, "Mama, look at me, I am White. I am White. Laughing, she says, "No more South Central for me. I want to shop and live up on Rodeo Drive in Beverly Hills with my blond hair and small nose."

Lakeesha's mother tells the Scientists, "Okay, she's White now. Just give us our money so we can get back to South Central. We got to get home before dark, cause if we don't, well—you know what they say, stray bullets have no name on them."

Scientist #1 tells his secretary, "Go ahead and escort them out and give them their checks."

"Oh yeah," says the mother, "Does anybody have cables, I need a jump start cause my car is parked outside and it ain't gonna start cause I need a new battery. We just barely made it here."

Rion and Sabrina start laughing.

Lakeesha says, "Hey, you Race Changers, I'm inviting all y'all up to my Penthouse at the Beverly Hills Hotel for Thanksgiving. The only thing you need to bring is some Blackeye peas and greens, but you have to make them like my Grandma makes them. They have to taste like soul food."

"Child, shut the hell up! You know this placed is bugged with microphones. Don't be telling them what we eat. They'll be wanting to steal that next," said Lakeesha's mother.

Reba looks at Sabrina and asks, "Is she acting part Black *and* part White?

Sabrina says, "I'm not too sure, but it sounds like she's just hungry."

Scientist #1 says, "Yes, yes, I like that. Talk about Beverly Hills and Rodeo Drive. And with your good looks, you are going to fit in very well in the White affluent world. This is going to be a good experiment."

"Everything is based on skin color and money. That's all they are talking about," said Reba.

"Maybe," I'm not sure at this point," says Rion.

"Listen everyone, before you go, I want you all to come into the next room, I have a surprise for you." says Scientist #2.

The Race Changers and the newly changed White girls and guys follow Scientist #2 into the next room. He brings out a silver box and opens it. He pulls out some gold necklaces and bracelets.

"What is all this?" asked Big Baby.

"This jewelry is made with a tracking device that will allow NASA to see how this experiment is going, to see if you all are acting White or Black, and if you folks are doing better in your new White life than you were in your past life as Black folks. Here, put them on," said Scientist #2. He hands a gold bracelet to Big Baby.

They new recruits all began putting on the jewelry.

"I don't know if I want to wear this." said Brady.

"It's either wear this or you get a chip implanted in the back of your neck," said Scientist #1.

"Uh, ok." said Brady.

David said, "I'll be glad to put this stuff on. Hey Brady, let's go to one of those uppity fancy restaurants tonight. This will give us a chance to test out our new look."

CHAPTER 4 In the Club – It's Not Funny!

A few hours later, the Race Changers arrive at a Florida night club. Life on Earth is about to get a little more confusing. They are waiting in line in front of the club with Solar Boy and Space Girl who have baseball caps on to cover their starch White skin color so as not to draw attention to themselves.

Rion is looking around and sees a familiar White guy also waiting in line. He yells, "Brady…Brady, is that you?" Sure enough, it was the two newly changed White guys, Brady and David. They were with two White girls, each of them had one on each arm.

Brady gets out of line and runs up to the Race Changers. Rion asks him, "How are things going for you being White now, Brady?"

"Great!" says Brady. I don't know what sad stories that young White college guys are talking about these days, but I'm having the time of my life! I'm loving this life! I got so many chicks—it's unreal. You will never believe what I'm going to tell you, man."

"What? What is it?" asks Reba.

Brady looks at Rion and says, "Hey man, let's step over there for a minute. I got something to tell you." Then he looks at the others and says, "Excuse us a minute, you guys." Then he walks with Rion about 5 feet away and whispers to him "Man, I never had so much ass before in my life!"

"What do you mean?" asked Rion.

This White thing ain't no joke! I mean the Sistas, when I was a Black man, those chicks had to play their games and pretend to be virgins or only have one guy or even make a brother wait months to hit that thang! You know, man. But now, with these White girls, they all want it after the first couple of dates."

"What?" says Rion.

"Yeah man, plus, they all think I'm super rich cause I'm White. I got more money now but I ain't rich, not yet anyway, but almost though. That's another plus, you got to try it Rion. It's a whole new way of life!"

"Well, you need to be telling all this to the Scientists. This is valuable information that they'd want to know for their research. The same goes for David.

"Yeah, but you know, since he's been White, I hardly ever see him. He's always on the way to some chick's house or to do a business deal. I'll get with the Scientists later, but for now this is the life for me. I don't ever want to go back to being Black. Nothing against being Black, but you know how that life can be, you're Black yourself."

"Now wait a minute Brady, you sound like a traitor – you are turning on your own Black race?"

"I am not Black, I am now White Brady Brandon, a distinguished Hedge Fund owner and I'll soon be worth millions of dollars."

"You see, Brady," says Rion, "you original Uncle Toms are all alike. You start making a little money and you change…whatever. I'll see you later man."

A half hour later, Rion and the other Race Changers are still standing in line waiting to get into the club. They notice the sky light up with nine UFOs hovering overhead. They shine bright lights from their ships on the people standing in line and through the windows of the twenty-six story building where the night club is located. Then out of nowhere appears this tall, skinny, Black guy standing in line about 10 feet behind them. He rushes to the front of the line ahead of the 500 people also waiting to get inside the club. He looks to be about 20 years old, and he's wearing thick-rimmed glasses and has long braided hair. He seems like he's kind of high, looking all wild-eyed.

Rion yells to the Race Changers, "Everyone stoop down, duck for cover. He might be working for Zardoff."

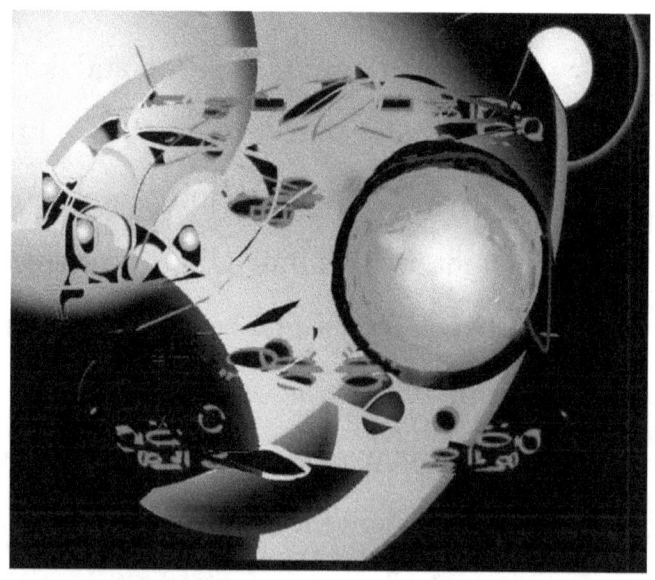

"What are those UFOs doing up in the sky?" asked Reba.

I don't know." answers Rion. "But they are probably up to destroying lives."

So they watch to see what's going to happen to this skinny Black guy who rushed the line. A big body builder type Black security guard approaches the young Black guy. Brady and David walk right pass everyone, their heads held high with their two White female guests. The security guards let them go right in.

Rion says to the Race Changers, You see how Brady and David got to walk in being White? Now watch what happens to the skinny brother with braids. I bet things are about to get ugly."

"What do you mean?" asked Reba.

"Just watch," said Rion.

The Security bouncer at the door says, "Hey man, you cut the line. You have to go."

"Who are you talking to? I was already here," said the Black guy angrily.

"Look at you," the bouncer said. "You must be on something cause you can barely stand up, noddin' and shit."

"I ain't going nowhere." Then he tried to go through the door. Another Security bouncer tried to stop him, so he took a punch at him, but the bouncer blocked his punch.

"Oh my gosh, a fight!" yells Zoey.

Reba says, "This is so stupid, why is he even trying to fight?"

Then the two Security bouncers wrestled the young brother down to the ground. He yelled at the bouncers, "You Uncle Toms, you ain't nothing but coons, you working for the White man. I'm gonna sue you!"

Two large White guys who were standing in line asked the two Security bouncers if they wanted them to kick the guys ass? Security told them, "No, but thanks."

Everyone in line watches in amazement. Even the street people begging for money stopped to laugh and cheer. The bouncers dragged the young Black guy down towards the end of the block, away from the club as he continued to yell.

Reba asked Rion, "What does the word coon mean?"

"Well Reba, I have to tell you that it's a derogatory name that was said to Black people during slavery times in the U.S.," said Rion. "When the word is used by Whites it translates to nigger. When used by Blacks it translates to Uncle Tom."

"What does Uncle Tom mean?"

"Uncle Tom means a Black man who is excessively obedient or subservient to White people."

The Race Changers are finally allowed to enter the club. Rion tells Solar Boy that the girls and Carlos are too young to be admitted into the club, so they must leave by 10 pm.

As they walk in together, Sabrina says, "Only non-alcoholic drinks for you teens, cause you're under age."

One of the managers in the club walks up to them and says, "Don't shake anyone's hand in here because there have been complaints from some of the patrons that after the UFO sighting and beams of light in the sky tonight, some people were approached by strangers who shook their hands in a weird way. These strangers would press their middle finger on the inside of their wrists where there pulse could be detected and then injected something into them with a small sharp object. Then they would start acting weird, saying racially derogatory words to others."

"That's what Zardoff did on another planet that he eventually destroyed," said Solar Boy.

"Okay, let's be careful Race Changers," said Rion, as he led the group further into the club.

The Race Changers are laughing and sighing from being on the run for so long, but that does not stop them from dancing. They really try to get Solar Boy on the dance floor because he looks like he's 14, but he has already lived for centuries. Ava asks Solar Boy, "How do you stay so young?"

Solar Boy responds, "I will tell you later."

The girls talk to their mothers and fathers on their cell phones. A couple of the Race Changer girls started crying from missing their families so much, but mostly they were laughing and talking about the exciting time they were having being together on this special journey.

Ava tells her mother, "This is a real adventure, Mom. I am living a sci-fi movie as we speak."

Ava's mother said, "Just be careful and remember you come from a family of Rabbis."

Their parents told them to keep studying and doing their homework online so that they will continue to get good grades in school. Reba and Zoey's mother told the girls that their Rabbi sent a message for them to keep going and not to stop, but to find a Temple to go to and pray on Shabbat, if they could, and to make sure they have their Shabbat dinner. Ava's mother told her to also try and keep a diary about this once in a lifetime adventure to save the world because it would be preserved in their family history and memorabilia forever.

The Race Changers are sitting at a table near the bar. There were flat screen TVs around the room so there was a lot going on. While they were waiting for the waiter to bring their food, Rion noticed there were three White guys sitting at the bar. One of them had a strange sounding voice. He looked like a wolf in the face and his hair was standing up over his head. He held up his cell phone and showed his two friends a video that he was looking at. They started laughing. The Race Changers could see it from where they were sitting. It was a video of a dark-skinned Black girl eating watermelon super fast with her large lips devouring it in seconds. They laughed and laughed. Then Wolfman got up and showed it to the White bartender and they both laughed together. Rion asked Sabrina, "Why is the bartender laughing with him?"

Sabrina said, "I don't know. Maybe he's just trying to get along with them because he's too embarrassed not to."

Reba said, "The nerve of them. What's so funny about that? Why are they laughing and making fun of that? I'm going to say something."

Rion said, "No, they are just entertaining themselves, but the stereotype of Black people eating watermelon is the reason why. Hell, everybody eats watermelon."

Noticing the frown on Rion's face, Reba asked, "Are they being racist Mr. Rion?"

"Maybe." said Rion, "But some of it stems from slavery days down South during the Civil War era. When we lived in Tennessee, my girls were 13 and 15 years old at the time. One day they wanted to eat watermelon on the front porch. We lived in a predominately White neighborhood. I told them 'No-sir-ee, you'll have to eat your watermelon in the backyard so your neighbors can't see you.' It just looks so countryfied when Black people eat watermelon on the front porch. I used to go to a White school and sometimes I would be the only Black kid in the cafeteria. I would be so self conscious when I chewed my food at lunch in the cafeteria because I felt like everyone was looking at my big lips."

Solar Boy said, "I've got something for them."

Rion said, "Are you thinking what I am thinking?"

"Yes," responded Solar Boy.

Solar Boy then pulled out his Race Changing machine and aimed it at the three guys at the bar, but he held it under the table and fired. Only one of the guys was changed to Black, the one that looks like Wolfman who was first watching the video and showed it to the other two guys. One of guys, half-drunk said, "Leo, what's going on here, have you taken Ecstasy or something because you are now Black."

"Who are you calling Black?" snapped Leo.

"You man! It must be something in them oysters that you ate cause you're as black as my shoes."

"Let's see them laugh now," Rion said.

The other Whites at the bar started laughing at Leo.

Solar Boy walked over to Leo, picked up his cell phone and then put it right back down. This time, the YouTube video showed him as a White guy eating watermelon real fast, but he was now a

Black man sitting at the bar looking at his White self inside of his own phone.

Rion says to Solar Boy, "That was genius, you are reversing the roles. I don't hear Leo laughing now." Leo jumps up and runs out of the club.

Reba started crying and yells out, "Why does it always have to be about race and color?" Then she jumps up and runs to the bathroom. Her sister, Zoey, runs after her.

Everyone is quiet for awhile as they pick at their food, having lost their appetites because of the watermelon video.

Sabrina says, " It's not just about race anymore—this thing is also about good versus evil. We now have White

Supremacists protesting against other races and other Whites protesting against them, along with Blacks, Muslims, Chinese, Spanish and new immigrants. It's really a crazy world we're living in now. And there's young male extremists committing violent crimes against others and themselves. I didn't grow up in a world like this.

Rion says, "You're exactly right, Sabrina. It's good versus evil and the race issue is inside of that."

Sabrina gets up and goes to the bathroom. She hugs Reba and wipes her tears away. "Why are you crying Reba?" asked Sabrina.

"I love Carlos the way he is now, but he's going to have to be changed to another person. He's going to be changed to a White guy, I just know it. I don't think that I'm beautiful enough for him. Look at my pug nose and my thin lips."

"Why do you say that? All the boys in your class like you. You're the 'it' girl. Didn't Carlos tell you that he loves you?"

"I know, but while we were on the dance floor, I saw him looking at that lady DJ and she was staring at him too. Her name is DJ Hot Pants. I googled her name and read some crazy stories about her."

"What kind of stories?" asked Sabrina.

"When she was in high school, she would take young guys home with her on the first date." I also heard that when she was in high school, she would stand outside of the cafeteria while 50 boys stood in line, and she would kiss them all, one by one. They would give her one dollar for one kiss. Supposedly, she saved up enough money to purchase a turntable and DJ equipment.

"Whaaat?" said Sabrina.

"Yep, she did that everyday for a week until her Homeroom teacher found out about it and told her parents. The rumor was that if any boy looked into her eyes while she was kissing them, he would become hypnotized and then fall in love with her. And then he would ask her to marry him right there on the spot."

"Don't you worry about Carlos, he just likes her because she's a little older than he is."

"But she has a better shape than me and she's more beautiful than me. She has fuller lips and big eyes. Look at me, I have auburn hair, and a few freckles and I'm practically skinny."

"Carlos is a fine gentleman and he will make the right choice, but at his age, most young boys at some time or another become infatuated with older women. Besides, you're too young to get so serious about any one boy. You've got a lot more growing and living to do before you are ready to settle down and get married. Now let's go back out there and get our dance on!"

So they go back out to the VIP lounge area and join the others. All of the Race Changers partied and danced and had fun for a while.

Reba asked Solar Boy, "Why don't you just make us all invisible and beam us into the White House or just fly us to Washington in your spaceship to meet the President? That way it won't be so hard on us."

Solar Boy answered, "For the same reason we walked in the desert in Nevada to get to Area 51 and Area 52. It's how the story of mankind is supposed to play out for people of Earth. For humans, when things come too easy, it doesn't mean much, but when things are difficult, it really makes it worth getting in the end. Your survival is worth having. I am happy to be a part of the Race Changers and so far it has been a joy ride for me. One day, I want to take all of you to see other planets, and the many wonders that exist in my galaxy."

Reba then asked, "Can we put the Israeli flag on a planet when we go there if it's not occupied?"

"Yeah," said Ava. "Let's build a Synagogue there!"

"I don't know," answered Solar Boy. "That decision would have to be made by the Lab Scientists and your Rabbi, and maybe your President too."

Three mean looking Asian men entered the club and spotted the Race Changers. They walked over to them. One of them said, "We are Korean government agents. Enjoy your lives young ladies while you can because it's going to be a different world come January 1st, New Year's day. I know that Solar Boy must have mentioned this before, but it's important for you to know that all of the NASA space news on TV and the internet, and all of the Scientists and Astronomers are talking about the Alien Invasion."

"They are really creepy," said Sharon. Then she started crying. " Being away from my family, I wonder if I'll ever see them again. Even if the invasion begins, and everyone has been changed to White, will my parents who are Jewish but look White, get changed to White again? Will they look completely different with different facial features? What if I don't recognize them and never see them again? Then what?

Sabrina says, "And what if I get changed from African American to White and Rion is not able to identify me, the love of his life, his soulmate, or if during this mission we get lost and he forgets my new White look?"

"Well, hold on now everybody," says Rion, "I think we are getting a little too carried away. Let's get back to the mission and try to stay focused and positive. We all have to stay dedicated and you girls, don't call or text your little boyfriends and girlfriends and talk to them every five minutes, and tell them our plans and how you miss them and all of that mushy stuff. I say that because I got word from Bill Diamond that he read in the newspaper that all of the CIA agents are on the lookout for us now, even agents from other countries and even the mafia, and major corporations working in cahoots with the mafia. Everybody wants us and especially Solar Boy because they want all of the secrets of energy and deep space since the beginning of our Universe. They believe he has it all stored inside of him or in his spaceship. In addition to that, he has the Race Changing machine. You know everybody wants that. Even some of those G's in the hood. So we can't stay here enjoying ourselves too long because we might get caught. Our phones might even be bugged. So I want all cell phones off, and don't turn them on to make any calls without my permission. I know that your parents want you to do your school work on the internet, but they don't have a clue what we are all really involved in. This is one time you won't get in trouble if you don't do your school work. We must be extremely careful at all times."

All the Race Changer girls and Carlos turn their phones off.

Suddenly, gunshots rang out in the club and everybody started running in all directions. Rion yelled, On the floor! NOW! Rion thinks, *I haven't had bullets whizzing by my ears in a long time.* Rion and Sabrina and the other Race Changers ran and rushed out of a back door into the alley where Mr. Diamond already had their Cadillac SUV waiting for them.

"Where is Reba and Zoey?" Ava asked.

Rion looked around, and then he pulls out two meteor laser Glock guns and tells Solar Boy "Come on, let's go back inside and get our girls. If we have to kill some bad guys to save them, then so be it."

Solar Boy takes one of the weapons and says, "Okay, let's go."

Rion told Sabrina and the rest of the Race Changers that they would be right back and to lock the doors to the SUV until they return. So they go back inside the club, but this time they enter through the front door. Solar Boy leads the way because he has vision that allows him to see in the dark. He gives Rion some glasses and tells him to wear them because if any bad aliens were in the club, the glasses would reveal them, and that they would look like hideous monsters. He tells Rion, "Don't let them touch you. If you see one, just shoot it with your laser gun." They walk down a long dark hallway. To the left they see lots of people lying on the floor and some leaning up against the wall. Rion spots three undercover bad aliens outside of the ladies' bathroom about to go in. Then he and Solar Boy hear calls for help from inside.

Rion shouts, "Its Reba!" He yells to her to get away from the door. Rion and Solar Boy begin to shoot their laser Glock guns at the aliens. They disintegrated into thin air leaving a puddle of green and purple slime on the walls and floor. Then he and Solar Boy step over the alien slime and open the bathroom door, grab the girls, and come out blasting all the way down the hallway as they run as fast as they can.

Zoey says "I can't keep up, my legs are tired."

Rion said, "Then I'll carry you." So he lifts her up and puts her over his left shoulder and continues to shoot his laser gun with his right hand. Reba yells, "The back door is blocked with tables and chairs stacked up against it!" Some of the night club's body guards are mafia hit men and they are running behind them shooting at them. Solar Boy aimed his meteor laser Glock gun at the wall next to the back door. He shoots a hole in it six feet high and six feet wide. They run through it into the alley, then jump into the SUV and speed away, barely escaping the mafia's bullets flying past them.

"My heart is beating like crazy, I can't take it," said Zoey. Sabrina takes some orange juice out of their cooler and gives it to Zoey. She starts to calm down.

Rion counts heads. "Wait!" he shouts. He comes to a screeching halt. "Where is Carlos?"

"Carlos!" screams Reba. "Where is Carlos?"

"I saw Carlos running out of the building into the alley. He was with some 21 year old looking lady with long hair and a tight fitting red dress on," Sharon said.

Rion said, "I remember now. I did see him running the other way when the gunfire started. I guess she called herself helping him to escape."

Reba starts crying, "I want Carlos back." The other girls try to console her.

"Okay," Rion says. "We'll drive around and try to find him."

CHAPTER 5 Carlos Runs Off with a Hot Chick from the Club

In the meantime, Carlos is riding in the car with the hot looking chick in the red dress. She pulls up to a mansion.

"Wow," he says. "Do you live here?"

"Yes I do," answers the lady. "We can rest here until the big fight in the club blows over."

"Okay," said Carlos, as they walk inside.

"I'll just put the chain on the door for safe keeping. Why don't you sit down and take your shoes off. I'm going upstairs to put on something comfortable."

"Oh sure, sure," says Carlos nervously. "I have to make a quick phone call. You go on up, I'll just be a minute."

He calls one of his best friends. "Hey, Arnaldo, it's me."

"Me?...Who?"

"Stop playing around man, it's me, Carlos."

"Carlos! Where are you man, the whole world is looking for you and the rest of your group."

"I know, I know, but listen. I got me a hot date. I am getting ready to get some ass, man!"

"Who is she?"

"It's this hot chick I met in a club tonight."

"Really man? Then go for it—why the hell are you calling me? Is she Hispanic?"

"Well, she kinda looks like she could be, or maybe Italian or something like that. Who cares anyway?" I'm just not sure if I should go through with it cause I love my Jewish girlfriend, Reba, and we promised we would be loyal to each other."

"Man, go ahead and ride her like a damn cowboy! My Uncle told me to get as many chicks as I can while I'm a young buck."

"I guess, but my conscious is gettin' to me."

The sexy lady calls downstairs to Carlos, almost singing the words to him. "Sweetie, I got something for you, but you have to come upstairs to get it."

"Coming," he yells back to her.

"Arnaldo, I am a man, so I am going to do what a man does. I'm still nervous, but here goes." He hits End Call on his cell phone and slowly walks upstairs, tripping on the first step. The gorgeous lady is standing by the bed in a sexy, black see-through nightgown. Her full figure-eight body is showing right through it.

"Wow," said Carlos. "You smell nice." Carlos is grinning from ear to ear like a kid in a candy store. "I'm getting kind of excited. Hey, my name is Carlos, what's your name?"

"What difference does it make what my name is?"

"Hell, none at all, forget it." Carlos looks around the room, "Wow, Miss, you have a lot of candles lit around your bed."

"I know, Baby, this will be a night you will never forget. Now, my sweet Carlos, why don't you take off all your clothes and get in bed with me? But first I need to handcuff you."

"What? Handcuffs?"

"Yes, honey." She kisses Carlos' forehead, then his nose, and then his lips.

"No, I need my hands free cause I'm going to make love to you with these magical fingers of mine." He wiggles his fingers in her face.

She lays down on the bed and then Carlos stumbles over his own feet and falls clumsily onto the bed beside her, giggling like a child.

"I want you Carlos." she says. She kisses him on the lips, ever so gently. He awkwardly tries to put his arms around her. He runs his fingers through her hair and all of it moves and shifts to one side. "What the hell?" said Carlos.

"Wait just a minute." she says, "I have to take my wig off." She gets up out of bed and puts her wig on the dresser and then gets back into bed. Her real hair is very short. Carlos tries to ignore it and focuses on her body. They begin to cuddle and kiss.

121

"Wow, you have a real sexy body Miss."

"Wait," she says. I have to take off my eyelashes." So she gets out of the bed again, showing her pretty legs and boobs, takes her false eyelashes off and puts them on the dresser next to her wig. Then she gets back into bed.

They hold each other and kiss some more. Once again she says, "Hold on Carlos, now don't let this freak you out, but I really do have to remove my left leg—well, only the bottom half. It's prosthetic."

Carlos's face has the look of terror on it. She gets out of bed, yet again, and loosens the screws that's attached to her left knee, and removes her leg from the knee down. She puts it up on the dresser next to her wig and false eyelashes. Once again, she hops back into bed and says, "Okay Baby, let's go, I'm ready!"

Carlos, totally frustrated and repulsed says, "Why don't I just get up on top of the dresser and make love to those female parts, cause lady, there's more up there than what's down here in bed with me."

The lady laughs wildly as if it turned her on to hear that. *She's turning into a freak instead of a rare hot date*, thinks Carlos. Suddenly, there's a loud knock on the door. BAM, BAM, BAM. Carlos jumps, "What is that?" he asked.

"Oh no!" the lady gasps. "My husband! Get your clothes on quick!"

"Husband? I didn't know you were married!"

"You didn't ask me. He's in the secret service and he's very jealous. He'll shoot and kill you and then hide your body so that nobody will ever find you."

"What the hell?" says Carlos. He quickly grabs his shoes and clothes that were lying in a pile on the floor. He tries to open a window but it wouldn't budge. He went to another window and was able to open it, but a screen was there.

The husband kicks the front door open and runs up the stairs yelling, "Whose here with my wife, I'll kill the bastard!"

"Oh, shit!" says Carlos. He punches out the screen, and takes one leap and was on the ground uninjured. He was grateful that his jump was only from the second floor because the huge mansion had five floors in it.

The lady yells to him, "Run, run, my husband is really jealous."

The husband runs into the room and over to the window and starts shooting at Carlos.

Carlos runs down the driveway to the street, naked, clutching his clothes and trying to cover his private parts at the same time. Out of nowhere a Cadillac SUV speeds towards him, tires screeching, then the front door on the passenger's side flies open. Rion yells, "Jump in, man!"

Carlos jumps in and slams the door shut as Rion speeds away.

Rion says, "I knew you couldn't be far from the club."

Scared and out of breath, Carlos says, "I'm so glad to see you, Mr. Rion. That chick's husband was going to kill me. He shot at me several times, but I remembered the tactical training you gave us in the desert that time, you said that when someone is shooting at you, to run zig zag."

I am an OG Carlos, you know, Original Gangster. I did the same stuff you're trying to do now except that I got the prize from the lady before her husband came home, back in the day—not like you, young blood." Rion tries to keep from laughing.

"Do I tell Reba?"

"No, my boy, you don't have to tell the woman everything, plus nothing happened, so there's nothing to tell. Just see this as a life lesson. So the moral of this story is don't fool around with married women. And remember to ask if they are married first."

Carlos is breathing hard and struggling to get his clothes on. "Yeah, yeah, okay, where are the others?"

"They checked into a hotel for some much needed R&R. Solar Boy and Space Girl are meeting with NASA to discuss a strategy for when the shit hits the fan with Zardoff. Hurry up and get your clothes on, we're going to pick them up now. Good luck with Reba." Rion starts laughing. "Man, I remember those days when I was your age."

CHAPTER 6 Notorious Alien Leader
Zardoff Invades DC

The Race Changers are now leaving
Florida and headed for Washington, DC.
They are driving north on Interstate
Highway 95. They stop off in Newport
News, Virginia to grab a bite to eat. Rion
suggests they go to see his and Sabrina's
best friends, Thad and Ruth Greer. Thad was
the best man at their wedding. The Greers
were thrilled to see them, and they knew
very well that their house was one place
where the government, reporters and Zardoff
couldn't find them. Ruth prepares a
wonderful meal for the Race Changers. Rion
and Thad play pool while Solar Boy
watches. They are talking and laughing
about the good old days when they worked
together at the Annie Mae company in
Washington, DC. Rion fills Thad in on the

latest about their mission while the others enjoy talking to Ruth in the kitchen. Ruth shares stories with them about Rion and Sabrina and Rion's climb to fame and fortune as a world famous international Artist, with Sabrina as his muse. The Race Changers spend the night at the Greers.

They wake up early and eat a good old country breakfast. They say good-bye to the Greers and then drive several hours to Washington, DC, talking and laughing all the way.

The Race Changers finally arrive in DC. They ride by the Washington Monument and the Capitol. The girls and Carlos were so amazed. Rion says, "It feels so good to be back in my hometown of Washington, DC where I grew up." I'm going to take you all to the National

Arboretum. Rion drives through the winding roads of the Arboretum between beautiful trees and flowers. They stop at a large pond with a white gazebo surrounded by all kinds of flowers.

"This is where Sabrina and I used to come and have picnics in the spring and summer."

Ava said, "This is a real magical place. I want my yard to look like this when I get married."

"Whose going to marry you, you old hag?" said Sharon. Then she starts laughing hysterically. "I'm just kidding Ava. I guess this whole ordeal of traveling around running from bad aliens is getting to me. As fun and exciting as it is, I'm way out of my comfort zone."

Sabrina said, "We can't lose our focus girls. Let's keep it together now."

Rion pulls over and parks. He says, "Let's get out and stretch our legs. We're all going to pull out our portable painting easels and canvases and I want a finished painting of this beautiful garden by this lovely pond within two hours."

"Two hours?" said the kids with surprised looks on their faces.

"Yes, two hours. We have to leave after that because as I remember from coming here as a kid, once they lock the gates at 5:00 pm, they let attack dogs loose—black and brown Rottweiler dogs. They roam these grounds looking for girls and boys to eat, so get to painting because we aren't leaving until you're done."

The Race Changers scurry along with their art supplies. Some sit in the gazebo, and some sit on the grass next to it. "It's fun to paint outdoors in nature. Just get started and remember to use lots of color, just like nature does," said Rion. So they paint and eat and laugh together, but soon all are quiet and concentrating on their paintings.

Reba and Carlos stray from the group. They walk a good distance away from them. They could easily get lost in the 446 acres of the National Arboretum. As they walk up a trail surrounded by pine trees, they can see the sun begin to set in the distance. They indulge in a kiss in the shadows of the trees.

"What do you miss most Carlos?" asked Reba.

"I miss my family the most," said Carlos. How about you Reba?"

"Well, I don't know, it's not so much about missing, it's just that I love you and I hope you don't have to be changed to look White."

"I'm going to wait until the last day to be changed. I know I'm a good looking Mexican kid, but I might go back across the border to Mexico to hide in a cave somewhere if these aliens are really coming. I'm sure that my family will do that, and I want to be with them. They might not want to be changed to another race. Will you still love me if I do have to become White, Reba?"

"I guess so, but I don't know what you would look like."

They both laugh.

"Will you still love me if I have to change my color," asked Reba?

"You are a pretty shade of White, like cream, so you might not have to get your color changed. Reba, you are my girl, my first love and my last love. There won't be anyone else that can even come close to taking your place." They hug and kiss. They have been away from the group now for more than two hours. "We have to go back now. Remember what Mr. Rion said about those vicious attack dogs running loose in here."

"Oh yeah. We didn't finish our painting either."

"Don't worry, I won't let anything happen to you. My father always taught me how to be brave and protect our women."

"I love you Carlos. Now let's start walking back."

Rion was driving the other Race Changers around in the SUV looking for Carlos and Reba. Right then, Reba and Carlos heard dogs barking. It kept getting louder and louder. Reba turns around and sees 4 Rottweiler dogs running towards them. So they ran. They try to outrun the dogs, but the dogs are gaining on them. Rion spots them and speeds towards them. Luckily, he reached them before the dogs did. They jumped into the SUV. Now they were safe.

The Cadillac SUV makes it through

the exit gate right before it closed.

"Honey, I'm getting kind of hungry," said Sabrina.

"Let's go to Eddie Leonard's Sandwich Shop," responded Rion. "This place has the best fish sandwiches and steak and cheese subs!"

"Great, I'm starving," said Sharon.

"Me too," said Ava.

"Do they sell cupcakes there?" asked Zoey.

They all burst into laughter.

Rion parks on Bladensburg Road and everyone gets out. As they walk along, they look to their left and see the Mt. Olive Cemetery across the street. It's dusk now and everyone is enjoying walking with no reporters or paparazzi or enemies on their trail. Reba looks up and says, "What is that?"

Then Rion looks up and says, "Zardoff is at it again!"

"Are you kidding me, Rion?" asked Sabrina.

"No, I'm not."

All the girls scream.

Now they can all see the sky with huge color holes that look like ripples. It was as if someone dropped a pebble into a water pond, or like someone was throwing buckets of paint into the sky. It would appear then disappear, and reappear again in another color.

Rion closed his eyes, then dropped to his knees and started praying. Sabrina knelt down next to him. People driving in traffic stopped and got out of their cars. Everyone was looking and pointing up at the sky. It was a busy intersection so people were honking their horns and rear-ending other cars due to the distracting activity in the sky.

Other people got on their knees too, and some people made the sign of the cross, and some were screaming and crying.

One man yelled, "They're here! The bad aliens are here, we're all doomed! We're all gonna die today."

Solar boy suddenly appears with Space Girl. Solar Boy said, "The bad aliens are running tests and checking things out

here. The last days here on Earth are getting very close. I will use one of my atomic laser guns to try and keep them from entering though the wormhole, but I don't know how long I can hold them off." Solar Boy flew 40 feet in the air and started shooting at the worm holes.

Then there were several loud explosions and about 8 of the red, blue, orange and yellow wormholes that were hovering in mid air all lined up horizontally. They began shooting out a light pink gas or some type of vapor because every one's eyes began to water excessively, and instead of their eyes getting smaller, they grew larger and they became very cold. Sabrina began to shiver so Rion drew her close and wrapped his arms around her. Then the real show began.

Appearing in the sky above them are several huge spaceships, starships, mother ships, and even giant size robots on flying iron-like horses with wings and bright, orange fire around them. They were all coming out of these wormholes plummeting at tremendous speed, so fast that it made everyone shake and shiver from the cold wind that was produced by all of the aircraft above them. Carlos put his jacket around Reba and the other girls clung to each other. Then one of the giant, shiny robots on its flying iron horse pointed its spear and shot towards the cemetery across the street. A huge blue lightning bolt struck the ground and made it rumble. The ground cracked open about a foot wide in the middle of the street on Bladensburg Road and there was a shrill sound like a banshee or coyote howling. It was so high pitched that the Race Changers and all the people who were gathered around them had to cover their ears. They were all so terrified that they couldn't even run.

"I can't move my feet," said Carlos. "I want to run buy my feet won't move."

Then the tombstones on the graves in

the cemetery started to move and now it was dark outside, but an orange light from somewhere in the sky shinned down on the graves and moved from tombstone to tombstone. People with decayed bodies in tattered clothing appeared and disappeared. Reba yells, "A Zombie attack!" The Race Changers and all the other people started screaming. Solar Boy and Space Girl just stood there unmoved. They've probably seen 10 times worst than this in their space travel.

Sabrina said, "Those must be lost souls escaping. Those bad aliens must be using them as another plan of attack."

All the Race Changers were huddled on the sidewalk shaking with terror because they didn't know what was going to come out of those wormholes in the sky, other than light. Rion says, "We're being attacked from above and below." Then the decayed bodies in the cemetery began to look through the rod iron fence at the Race Changers. They began to climb over it. Some of the zombies walked right through it. Sabrina pointed at them. Rion grabbed her hand and said, "Don't ever do that. The old folks say to never point your finger at a cemetery or you'll loose it." Flashes of different color lights were so bright that it was almost blinding.

The iron horses, robots and spaceships were flying very low over their heads. They had to duck to keep from being hit by them.

Many people ran into stores to hide and others just left their cars in the middle of the street and made a big pile-up mess. Others got on top of their car, gazing upwards.

Rion said, "My eyes can't believe what I am seeing. I thought they said the invasion wasn't going to happen until January 1st. Solar Boy saw some of the zombies from the cemetery walking towards them. He told the Race Changers not to stare at them because if they did, they would turn into a zombie and fall in love with them.

"Who wants to love a zombie anyway?" said Reba. They are so disgusting!"

"Just don't look them in the eye. Here, put these solar moon glasses on and they will protect your eyes," said Solar Boy. He handed Reba the glasses.

Some of the zombies jumped aboard the subway train and headed to downtown DC. They even took over the train and began driving it. Then they turned off the lights after they went underground and began to beat up and bite people.

Other zombies carjacked some vehicles, waving their arms out the windows yelling, "What are you looking at? You haven't seen a dead person before?" Some were even riding on the hoods of cars laughing wildly. Then several car loads of zombies took their skulls off and rolled them through the crowds of families and kids standing on the corners at intersections watching in terror. Immediately the crowd screamed and ran away from the skulls. Then the skulls started talking crazy and chasing the people running, even though they had no bodies attached to them. Some even threw their nasty decayed heads and crashed out store windows.

Now here comes about 30 street dudes from Trinidad near Neal Street running from around the corner with baseball bats.

"Look, look!" shouted Reba. "They are kicking and beating the crap out of those aliens and zombies."

"Good," said Zoey.

Then about 70 more people showed up. Some ran to the scene and others jumped out of five vans that just pulled up.

"Damn!" said Rion, "It's the notorious badass Rosedale Gang." Those guys started shooting their guns at anything moving. Some of them did drive-bys and shot at the alien spaceships, ghosts, and whatever else that looked sinister.

Sabrina yells, "Those gang guys have machetes and butcher knives and two of them has a zombie pinned against a fence."

"Look, Race Changers, that's what these guys do in the hood everyday, all day," said Rion. "I'm glad they are on our side. I had to go to school with these gangs. But I survived. It just made me tougher."

"Watch out!" yells Reba. There's a UFO alien spacecraft coming down, about to crash. Move, move, get out of the way!"

The Race Changers quickly change locations. There is smoke and fire everywhere and people are yelling.

These ghoulish zombies drove the jacked cars superfast down Highway 95

North towards New York, and some took Highway 95 South towards the Southern states. "It looks as though the invasion is officially happening," said Solar Boy. He tells the Race Changers that he and Space Girl are going to their spaceship and finish those ghosts and zombies off. Once inside their spacecraft, Solar Boy waives his hand and says some magical words. Then Solar Boy presses a button and a blueish-green light starts flashing on the right arm of his space suit. Out of nowhere a magical chest appears and is spinning in the air inside the spacecraft.

Meanwhile, the Race Changers are huddled together on the sidewalk, still shooting their laser weapons at the zombies above and below at the cemetery but are almost losing the battle against the invasion. Rion says, "Our weapons seem like they are useless against these zombies, But I think I've found the answer. I just made a call to our military at the Pentagon to send some jet drones to fly over here and shoot flames of fire into the cemetery and at those escaped zombie ghosts. Look—pointing up— here they come now, it must be about 20 or 30 of them."

The Air Force drones fly low and shoot red liquid, lava-like rays into the cemetery. Some of the zombies fall and then catch on fire. They can barely move with the liquid fire weighing them down. But more of them just keep coming from under the ground in the cemetery. It's like a bottomless well. They are laughing wildly. Some of them even take off down M Street and run into some of the homes, then catch fire immediately upon entry.

"Damn, what do we do now?" asked Rion. The Air Force drones fly off into the horizon towards New York Avenue following some of the other zombies, and blasting them with flames of fire.

"This is like watching a horror movie with me in it." said Sharon.

Solar Boy, still hovering in his spacecraft above, reaches into the magical chest and pulls out a special rock, but not

just any rock, it's a piece of asteroid from the Big Bang. It has magical powers. It's glowing and pulsating. Solar Boy, with the stone in his hand, raises both of his arms above his head and creates another wormhole in the sky that looks so different from the ones earlier.

Out of this new wormhole comes spaceships flying at a high rate of speed towards the zombies that are still coming out of the cemetery. These spaceships are from the army of Solar Boy's own galaxy, Andromeda.

Ava begins to cheer and yells, "We are rescued!" The Race Changers hug each other thinking that it's finally over.

These warriors begin to shoot and destroy the zombies and ghosts with their special weapons and literally kick the daylights out of them. But now there is chaos amongst the people. Homes are on fire, gas lines are exploding, stores are being vandalized, cars at the intersection of Bladensburg Rd and Mt. Olive Rd., Northeast are running into each other because the traffic light is out, and there are some Black and White people actually fighting each other. It's hard to tell if it's a racial fight, or a self-defense fight, or if people are just in shock from being terrorized by zombies and ghosts coming out of the cemetery, or all of the above.

Some Black girls come walking down the street with tight jean shorts on popping gum. They just walk right past the cemetery like nothing was going on. One of them says to the others, "Girl, I'm going to the club to get my drink on. I can watch this shit on the news any day."

"I don't know how they can do that," says Sabrina.

"I don't know either," says Zoey.

"I do," Rion says. "Hell, this type of chaos and crap goes on every day in the hood."

Carlos asks, "Mr. Rion, how do we stop all the chaos going on with all the people now?"

"Yeah, Sweetheart, have we really been successful if we can stop zombies from killing people but then turn around and watch people kill each other instead?" said Sabrina.

Rion says, "There are a lot of lessons to be learned from today. But we can't talk now. We'll discuss them later."

Reba shouts, "I know— I'm gonna call my Uncle Bill Diamond to see if he can help." The Race Changers all agree it's a good idea to reach out to him.

Reba calls him and he answers, *"Bill Diamond in the rough speaking."*

"Hi Uncle, it's your niece, Reba."

"Hey sweet niece, are you okay? Is Zoey okay?"

"We're fine—sort of. Are you busy right now Uncle Bill?"

*"I'm having lunch with the
Ambassador of Sweden at the Swedish
Embassy on Massachusetts Ave."*

"Well, these Aliens, you know—the
bad ones—they have a full scale attack
going on here in Washington, DC, and they
are really making a mess out here."

"What do you need me to do?" asked
Bill.

"Not sure," says Reba. "We are losing
the battle. There are zombies, aliens and
ghosts. Some are flying from the sky
through wormholes and others are coming
out of a cemetery here."

Bill says, *"I hear all of that darn
shooting and explosions in the background.
Those sorry shooters can never hit the target*

anyway. I got it. I know just what to do. I will take the Ambassador's helicopter to you my precious one. Now don't you worry one bit. I am on the way and when I get there I am going to kick some aliens' asses, big time!"

"Okay Uncle, but hurry."

Bill Diamond takes a sip out of his gold goblet and toasts with the Ambassador and others and says, "I have to save the world, again." The audience of dignitaries and world leaders beg Bill to tell them what happened before when he saved the world. But he stands up and walks across the room as three gorgeous women in gowns are clamoring all over him, begging him not to leave. He asks the Ambassador if he could borrow his helicopter and his pilot. And of course, the Ambassador was accommodating. Then he and the pilot leave and jump in the helicopter and take off. They are now airborne and the women are on the ground looking up begging for Bill to return. He just blows them a kiss and leans out of the window and yells, "Keep it warm till I return, and you know what I mean too!"

They yell back to him, "For you, Bill, anything."

Bill is now flying over neighborhoods in DC. From the helicopter, he calls Luce, his maid at his ranch in Pahrump, Nevada and explains to her the Alien battle that is happening in Washington, DC right now. She told him that her son, Claude, told her months ago some government secrets he found out about at Area 52 involving space visitors from other worlds, and that one in particular might be able to save the Race Changers in DC.

"By golly, spit it out, woman. There is not a second to waste. What did he tell you?" asked Bill?

*"Well, when he was working in Area 52, one of the scientists who really liked Claude said to him, 'I am giving you some top secret information just in case Area 52 is ever destroyed by some type of attack—this could help save the planet and I want you to have it. I trust you but don't share this with anyone else, except in the event of an attack by aliens.' Claude agreed. Then the young scientist went on to explain to him that there was a Top Secret Government Project called, 'Alien Go Home' and that he and other scientists there invented an **Alien Nerve Gas.** He said that it could only slow*

down and freeze the aliens' movements for about 15 minutes. Then they would return to normal and be able to move freely again."

"This must be one of the reasons so many agents are after Claude because of what he knows," said Bill. Dog-gone-it, this is great my dear Luce. Do you know where I can get my hands on that stuff?"

"Yes, he stored it away in the storage shed here in the back-yard area."

"Great, so tell the Butler to go out there and find it."

Luce says, *"The Butler is on vacation in Hollywood, Mr. Diamond."*

"That crooked nose sorry ass Butler is never around when you need him. Then have my foreman load it up and sit it outside in the front circular driveway, and I will have Solar Boy fly it to me through a wormhole here in DC.

"Yes sir, right away, Mr. Diamond."

The Alien Nerve Gas arrives via wormhole in DC. Inside the box carrying the nerve gas was three spears. The nerve gas must be loaded into these spears in order to shoot the gas out onto the aliens, zombies and ghosts. After Bill arrives on the scene, he loads one of the spears with the nerve gas and begins to shoot. The aliens slow down and then stop moving. As Bill continues to shoot the spear, more and more aliens freeze.

"Look," says Reba, it's slowing them down.

"Yeah," says Zoey, but there are still more Zombies coming out of the cemetery and aliens are still coming out of that open wormhole in the sky. What are we going to do?"

"Keep fighting for now," says Rion. "Reba and Carlos, you two load up the other spears and keep shooting at the bad guys. We can win this battle but we need a miracle."

Rion whispers to Sabrina, "I hope I live to see my old house one more time." He points, "It's a few blocks up the street that way."

Sabrina says, "Don't worry honey, your ancestors are here fighting with you. Even though you can't see them, they are here with you in spirit."

Rion kisses Sabrina on the cheek.

Hundreds more of Zardoff's alien spaceships come flying out of the different color wormholes. The wormholes keep going in and out, and the alien spacecraft keep appearing, then disappearing into the night sky.

Reba says, "I love my Uncle. He's a winner and he has a lot of courage."

Zoey says, "Yeah, and we can't die now because I have never been to the White House, I want to see the President. Mom tells me all the time that you Sis, probably got your courage and nerve from Uncle Bill."

Solar boy contacts Bill Diamond on his cell phone. Bill puts him on speaker so the Race Changers can hear. He says, "I am running out of power for my Space Laser Ray gun. I need you to go to the Langston Golf Course and go to the 9th hole, dig 6 feet down and get the red ruby crystals that has been buried there since Earth was formed. It has magical powers and will restore all of my weapons' energy and firepower."

Rion says, "We can't go because Zardoff has shut down all of the electricity and power in the city. No cars can move, nothing."

Rion then yells to the gangs that are fighting, "Hey you Rosedale, Trinidad and Langston Terrace gangs, even you Bronsteins, and you Jewish guys from the Baltimore Delicatessen, listen up, I'm your

home boy, and we need transportation—
somebody go and get us some horses from
the Arboretum."

Sabrina says, "They're not going to
listen to you Rion, they are already out of
control."

"We'll just keep shooting that nerve
gas with those laser weapons."

About 10 minutes later, here comes
some of the gang members riding horses
towards them.

Sabrina says, "Whaaat? I don't
believe it."

Rion smiles and says, "Once a home
boy, always a home boy."

The three gang members dismount and then Bill Diamond and Rion mount the horses. Rion sees that there is a third horse and asks, "Do you know how to ride a horse, Reba?"

"You bet I do," said Reba.

"Then let's go, mount quickly."

Reba mounts the horse, then smiles at the other Race Changers. Carlos blows her a kiss.

Rion says, "Follow me, I know where the Langston Terrace Golf Course is. I used to go to Brown Jr. High and Charles Young Elementary right across the street from there."

They gallop pass dead zombies and people lying on the sidewalk, and cars burned up and overturned in the street. They

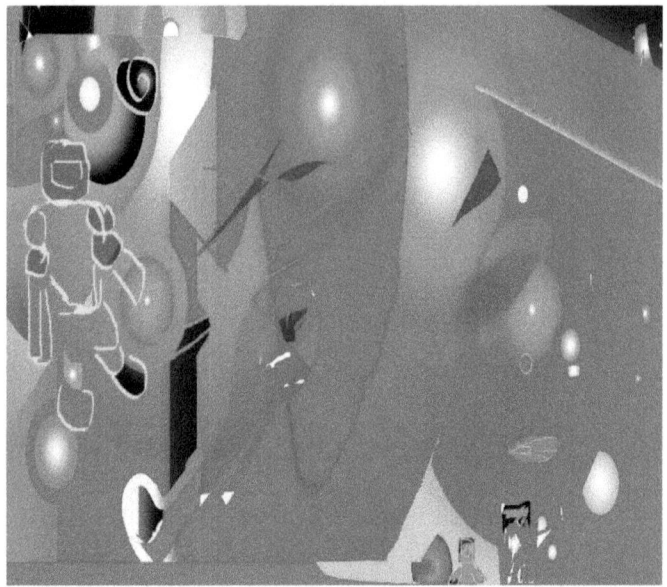

jump over them and keep galloping faster and faster. Then there is one alien spaceship that is chasing them. They gallop faster and faster.

Rion spots an enemy spaceship and shoots at it with his alien nerve gas laser spear. The ship slows and then stands still in the air. It wobbles and falls to the ground. It crashes into an eight-story apartment building and catches fire and kills several people. Then they see some of the ghosts and zombies carrying dead bodies out of the building. They fly them back to Mt. Olive Cemetery and then drag them underground into some of the graves.

Reba yells, "I don't believe what I am seeing. This is some scary stuff."

Rion yells back, "See it but don't see it, Reba. Ignore it for now."

Bill Diamond yells, "Okay everybody, let's keep going, we are on a mission you know, and don't ride in a straight line in case alien ships start chasing us again."

They continue to gallop fast through the streets of Northeast DC. When they get to the golf course, Bill Diamond yells, "Hee haw, Bill Diamond to the rescue. You aliens and zombies can kiss my rich fat ass." He waives his cowboy hat up in the air and leans forward galloping like a jockey pro. They find the 9th hole, dig up the stones and put them in their pockets. Then they take off again on their horses. They gallop even faster on their return, anxious to get back to the others. They give the stones to Solar Boy. He takes them to his spaceship.

Sabrina asks Reba if she was okay. Reba said, "It was fun, but very dangerous."

Bill Diamond kisses his nieces good-bye. "Keep me posted now. I have to get back to my ladies in waiting. Call me anytime. May love prevail." He jumps in the helicopter with the pilot who was waiting for him, and off they went.

CHAPTER 7 Lessons from the Hood

"Let's ditch these horses and try to make a run for it to my old house on K Street since things have simmered down a bit," said Rion.

"How long will it take us to get there?" asked Reba.

"About 15 minutes."

"Is it safe for us to walk there, Rion?" asked Sabrina.

"Actually, no. Those damn aliens are everywhere. They have injured and killed lots of people from my community here in Northeast. I am very sad about it."

"What about the invisible cloak!" asked Reba. "Its in the chest, right Solar Boy?"

"Yes," Solar Boy replied. Then he magically lowers the twirling chest from the air. No one can ever see it as long as it's covered with the purple cloak. He looks at Reba and says, "Go ahead, Reba, open it and pull out the purple cloaks."

"Hurry!" says Zoey, do what he says.

Reba opens the chest and very strange mathematical equations and symbols never seen before slowly rise up out of it. They could sense the energy emanating from it. She reaches inside the chest and pulls out several purple cloaks, one for everybody. She hands them out to the Race Changer group."

Solar Boy says, "Now put them on and Rion, you lead the way to your house. No one will be able to see you as long as you have these purple cloaks on. But let me warn you all of one thing. These cloaks have had magical powers since the beginning of time. But these powers will fail you if for one second you think doubt, fear, negativity or anything that is evil. If you do, you will no longer be invisible and the enemy will see you and capture you."

"Oh damn," says Reba, I'm not sure if I can think positive for 15 whole minutes."

"You all must train yourselves to do this. This is your first real inner space test. If you pass this one, we will go to other galaxies in space together. But we must learn this now. You only have one chance to learn it, so lets be safe and stay positive and invisible. Now grab your gear and put the cloaks over your heads, and walk one behind the other," said Solar Boy.

"I will lead. I know the way without even looking. Now lets go!" says Rion.

With the purple cloaks covering the Race Changers' heads, each one put their right hand on the right shoulder of the person in front of them with their heads down. In only a couple of minutes, 10 alien zombies with their weapons out come walking fast towards them.

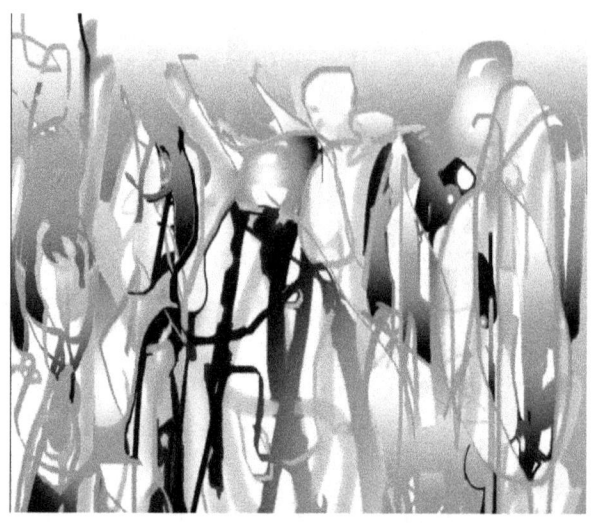

The alien zombie Captain said, "Where did they go? I just saw them."

The Race Changers keep walking until they reach Rion's old neighborhood. After 15 minutes they are now in the alley that leads to the back of Rion's old house.

Explosions are still happening and

police helicopters are flying overhead still battling the enemy.

Rion asked, "Is everyone okay? You can take your invisible cloaks off now. We made it. I bet you all were surprised that you could actually go fifteen minutes thinking only positive thoughts, and without fear.

"I had to think of funny stuff the whole time to keep from being afraid," said Zoey."

"Me too," said Carlos.

Sabrina said, "Rion, I thought about the first time we met. It was so special."

"Thanks, honey," responded Rion. "I thought about us traveling in space together and how our love would grow with each planet we visited." He kisses Sabrina on the lips.

Zoey says, "It's real scary around here Mr. Rion. I don't know how you survived growing up here."

"I learned how to adapt and survive and you can too. Remember that girls, and Carlos."

"Sure, okay, all that sounds good, but look over in the other direction. Am I seeing things? I think I see some more UFOs," said Reba.

"Where is Solar Boy and Space Girl?" asked Ava.

"They've disappeared again," said Sharon.

"They know we're meeting with the President tomorrow, so they'll be there, I'm sure of it. Get your weapons ready everybody," says Rion. "No talking and no giggling. Don't make a sound."

"Will do," says Sharon, as she turns here head towards Zoey. "No farting either."

The girls start laughing. Zoey takes a bite out of a smashed cupcake she found in the bottom of her backpack. "I'm so glad I found this. It tastes so good."

"Get serious!" yells Rion. "Be ready to fight in case we get ambushed. Let's all climb up in this big tree. We'll hide out until it gets darker, and then we'll sneak up the alley into my old house a few feet away."

"But I'm still hungry," cried Zoey,

"Does anybody have any cupcakes? Besides, I have to go to the bathroom."

Reba said, "Mom always said you were full of it, and she was right. You eat those cupcakes and then it all wants to come out of you a few minutes later. Just hold it in girl till this danger blows over. When Mr. Rion gets us some food, maybe he can buy you some cupcakes at the store that I saw down the street."

"Okay Sis, I'll try."

Rion, I'm too tired to even be afraid right now. And I think that's why no one is trying to notice any more UFOs," said Sabrina.

They all fall asleep on the huge tree limbs they perched themselves on. Its completely dark now, and shadows of huge flying saucers roll over their faces. Then a spacecraft lands nearby and disappears into the ground.

After a couple of hours, Rion wakes up everyone. Carlos helps Sabrina and the girls climb down out of the tree. Sabrina asks Rion, "Are you sure you made an appointment with the President, honey?"

"Yes," Rion says. "I hit him up on Twitter and he said to come by tomorrow to the east gate. He gave me a passcode to show the guards and said that his assistant would let us in."

"You hit the President up on Twitter, just like that?"

"Yep, I sure did. Look, I got

connections. I'll tell you about it later Babe. Right now we've got to get out of this alley."

They all walk down the alley.

As they walk, dogs start barking and helicopters are battling alien spacecraft above, shooting back and forth. Laser rays and bullets are hitting the ground close to them.

Rion yells, "Run, everybody run!"

When they finally reach the back of Rion's old house, they take cover under the back porch steps to catch their breath.

"I'm so excited about going to the White House," says Sharon.

Rion says, "Okay girls, its dark and dangerous around here, so I don't want any of you young ladies wandering off again." Just as he said that, they could hear automatic gunfire not too far away.

"What is that?" asked Reba.

"I told you this is a dangerous neighborhood. It ain't Alabasas or East Hills, California."

I know, but it just seems like there's hate and evil everywhere, no matter where you are or what race you are. One day when I was in the Mall with some friends, a White girl said to me, 'What's up Jap?' "I said, Jap?" She said, 'Yeah Jap—Jewish American Princess! Aren't you a Jew girl?' "I don't know how she could tell I was Jewish with my dark red hair. Maybe it was my nose."

Then Ava said, "That's odd because I always get the opposite. When I tell people I'm Jewish, they always say that I don't look Jewish. I tell them I'm a Persian Jew, and then they say, 'Oh, I couldn't tell because of your golden skin tone.'

Rion says, "To answer your question about the loud gunfire, I don't know if that's some of the boys in the hood or the National Guard fighting off the aliens. Remember when we were battling Zardorff in Vegas? When it comes down to humans fighting for mankind against bad aliens, the dudes in the hood and the good guys, and the US military will join forces and fight together. It's a new day. We should be pretty safe here because we'll have Solar Boy's robot guard dogs in the front and back yards patrolling. They will eat anything all at one time, bones, skin, everything.

After the gunfire subsides, they all come out from under the stairs. Rion and Carlos pull off planks from one of the windows in the back of the house. They climb in first to see what condition the house is in, then they help Sabrina and the girls climb through. They try to get comfortable on some old blankets they found on the floor and in the closet.

Sabrina says, "God! It smells terrible in here. Rion, you know how I hate bad odors. I think I'm going to throw up."

All the Race Changers jump back away from Sabrina after she said that. Rion opens the water bottle he pulled out of his pocket and quickly shakes some of the water in her face. "Rion!" screams Sabrina, what are you doing?

"You said you were feeling sick, Babe. I was trying to help you."

"Could you first let a Sista know before you drown her ass?"

"I'm sorry, Baby, it bothers me when you don't feel good."

"I know Sweetheart. How does it feel being back in the house you grew up in?"

"Well, a lot of my childhood memories are coming back. I remember my father sitting over there in his armchair— pointing— reading the paper, and my mother would be preparing dinner in the kitchen. I felt so good watching them and feeling so much love for them, and I still feel love for them now, even though they have passed on."

"You know what?" asks Sabrina. That's one of the things I love about you. You are so nostalgic."

Right then, they hear a knock on the door.

Rion whispers, "Don't open it!" He peeks through the venetian blinds and sees a lady holding a picnic basket. He recognizes her and opens the door.

Sabrina runs to the bathroom and throws up. Everyone holds their nose and Carlos says, "What is that smell?"

"Carol! you're Carol Hooper! Come

in," says Rion. They hug each other. "How did you know we were here?"

Carol says, "Well Rion, you're not exactly living a private life. I've been keeping up with you all on the news. And to be honest, it crossed my mind when I heard you all were in DC, that you might try and return to your old neighborhood to hide or something. I'm on your side, and I want to help you Race Changers any way I can. I'm as afraid as everyone else. Here—handing Rion the picnic basket—I brought you some food. I figured you all might be hungry. I wonder why it smells so foul outside."

Rion takes the basket from Carol and says, "Thanks, Carol. That smell you asked about is from dead zombies that the police and the military have killed. The only way to kill a zombie is to stab it or shoot it in the head, unless you have a laser weapon. They start decaying fast."

"I see. You know I still live in this neighborhood, two houses down. I'm the only one who never moved away. I remember when I used to baby sit you. I know that was a long time ago. I got two grandkids now. They're both grown. I wish you could meet them. Stuff has really changed. There's still a lot of automatic gunfire when the sun goes down coming from the Trinidad area and around the corner on L Street. I don't know why I never moved away. I guess cause it's home."

Sabrina comes out of the bathroom. "Carol, this is my wife, Sabrina."

"Hi Sabrina," says Carol. "Nice to meet you."

"Hello Carol," says Sabrina.

"Likewise."

"She's not feeling too well," Rion said. She's extremely sensitive to odors and with the smell of this boarded up house and the stench of dead zombies—well—you know." He hands the picnic basket to Sabrina and she hands it to Reba. She touches her stomach as if she might throw up again at the thought of food.

Reba said, "Miss Carol, what is it like living in this neighborhood now?"

"Well, its got two sides to it," said Carol. "A lot of foreigners moved in with money and Whites too. That made the property values go up for homes. This house, Rion, that your parents used to own, well it's going for almost a million dollars today. And down the street on H Street where everyone used to go and shop on Saturdays—it's almost like shopping in Georgetown or Beverly Hills! No more burned down, run down store fronts from the 1968 riots when Martin Luther King Jr. was assassinated. It's all changed now. I bet you didn't even recognize the area when you first drove in. It's no more an all Black neighborhood."

"Wow! I can't believe that this is the future I imagined when I was a kid," replied Rion. "When I was a kid sitting in class one day at Brown Jr. High School, I looked out the window and imagined seeing a flying saucer on the horizon, and now here they are, flying over the city. And the future is now. I loved this neighborhood then, but deep down inside I knew it could be so much better, and now it is, and I'm all grown up."

"That's amazing Rion. Why don't you all eat up, there's plenty there in the basket."

"Oh goody, I'm starved," said Sharon. Reba handed out sandwiches to everyone. The girls just held their sandwiches but didn't eat them. Ava handed her sandwich to Rion. He opened it up and looked between the two pieces of bread.

Rion said, "Thank you so much Carol, but the girls can't eat these sandwiches because they're made with ham. The girls are Jewish and it's against their faith to eat pork."

"Oh, I'm so sorry," says Carol. I can whip up something else real quick."

"Don't trouble yourself Carol. Is that Baltimore Delicatessen around the corner still there? I know that Jews used to own it and sell Kosher food there."

"Yes, after all this time, it's still there. Rion, you know I have two grown boys now. They just got back from Afghanistan and they know how to shoot to kill so they will be watching closely in case any zombies or aliens try to come through and attack from the back alley."

In the distance, they hear explosions and gunfire and helicopters with bright search lights. "I guess it's really on now," says Zoey.

"Yep, you're right, Zoey" says Sabrina.

"Thanks again, Carol, for the sandwiches—sorry the girls couldn't eat them. You better get home now while you still can. There's crazy and dangerous things going on out there."

"Okay," said Carol. Sabrina and the girls hug Carol, then she leaves.

Rion stands guard looking out the front window of the house with his finger on the trigger of his laser gun. He sits down in an old dusty chair that his father used to sit in all the time. He nods off a little. The others make beds on the floor with the old blankets they found.

About an hour later, they are all asleep. Reba sits up quickly. "I hear something?" she utters, wondering if she was dreaming or not. She's not sure if she was dreaming or not. "I think someone's at the door trying to get in. We forgot to lock the door." She jumps up and runs towards the door but trips and falls on a throw rug. She hits the floor hard. Then she covers her eyes because she knows that at this time of night no human would be out with all the chaos going on in the city and neighborhoods. Rion and the others are so tired they don't even wake up. Reba gets up off the floor and goes over to the window next to where Rion is sleeping. She peeps out between the venetian blinds and sees a tall dark being on the front porch. She senses that it's not human, but that it's something evil. *Is it one of the Kings of the Zombies?* she thought. The being is pacing back and forth on the front porch. It has small red lights at the back of its knees, and has long black hair all over its body. It's head is cone shaped and black also. *Oh my gosh, it's starting to turn around and look at me, I can't bear to watch it. I can feel it's evil and its trying to communicate with me to unlock the door.* She screams, "No, no! Help me Zoey! Mr. Rion, help!"

Rion jumps up and jerks open the door and aims his laser gun at the being.

It's Carol Hooper again. She's holding some packages.

Rion says, "Carol! I could've shot you, is everything okay? Hurry inside."

Everyone is awake now. Carol rushes in and says, "I had one of my sons go and get some food from the Jewish Delicatessen. I couldn't bear to think of you girls starving."

The girls take the food from her and thank her. They are so happy to finally have some food. As they all sit down to eat on the living room floor, Zoey asks Carol a question. "Mrs. Hooper, you grew up in this neighborhood which was all Black back then, but you look more White than Black. You could be White or Jewish or Spanish just by the way you look."

"I know," said Sharon, "But I'm a light-skinned Black person, like Sabrina."

"What was it like back in the day for you going to an all Black school in the hood?"

"Child, I tell you—it wasn't easy for me. A lot of the Sistas were jealous of me and said I thought I was cute. They were jealous because all the guys liked me. So what I did was, I went out and got me the

197

biggest, Blackest soul brother in school. He became my boyfriend and walked me from class to class and then home from school every day. Nobody ever messed with me after that."

"Wow, so it was hatred for you even within your own race, even in the hood?"

"Yeah girl, it sure was. Even today, I just act my race and not my color, because it's my culture, not my skin that makes me who I am. Now, if I go to a job interview, well, I have to act White then. Let me make myself clear, I have to talk White, not be White, so that they can relate to me."

"Interesting." said Zoey.

The other girls chimed in, "Yeah, that's real interesting."

Rion says, "You girls are getting a real life lesson from a pro here of how to survive as a person from the hood."

CHAPTER 8 The White House Meeting with the President and Race Changers

The next day, the Race Changers, Solar Boy and Space Girl are sitting in the Oval Office inside the White House along with three CIA bodyguards waiting for President Klump to come in. Finally, he walks in. "I know you all came a long way," says the President.

"Yes we have," says Reba. We have been all over the world and battled the Aliens, and not just bad aliens—well, we've been fighting everybody, Sir."

"I've been following you over the news, and my Agents have been keeping an eye on you too! I have decided to include a special vote this election year, and let the American people decide if they want all people of color to be changed to the White race to keep planet Earth from being destroyed by bad aliens.

"What the hell?" mumbles Rion. "Uh, Mr. President, with all due respect, don't you think that they will turn it down, even if it will save our planet from being destroyed?"

Ignoring Rion, the President says, "Also, I am going to sign a bill to have NASA build Wormhole Walls in Outer Space. These walls will only allow certain types of aliens to come through and enter Earth. I will have control over who comes in and who goes out of these Wormhole Walls in Space. If a space traveler does not look right or they dislike me, then they won't get in or out of Earth's atmosphere."

"But Mr. President, don't you want space explored and don't you want contact with good aliens?" asked Solar Boy.

"Yes, but I have to control it all. I control everything. You guys don't know that by now? I'm going to put together a Galaxy Army so that we can control outer space."

Solar Boy levitates to the ceiling and the CIA body guards get nervous and put their hands on their guns. "Calm down, everyone," says Rion. "He's an alien also. But he's a good alien. He's here to help us. You are going to need more than a wall in outer space to keep the billions of other alien life forms from entering Earth."

"What? I don't believe you," said the President. Then he tells the White House

Butler to pour him some Cognac. "Well, when they come, let them come. We'll just build detention centers for them and lock them all up."

Solar boy says, "That is not the answer. I need you to let me talk to NASA to help with lots of secrets for interplanetary travel and the ability to live forever and also the ability to change the color of peoples' skin.

President Klump says, "I can't wait to tell the world that two Aliens came to the White House and told me that we are going to be invaded by racist White aliens, and so all Black people or people of color have to be changed to White. Shit, they won't think twice about impeaching me then. They might even cancel my twitter account." He laughs. "I can't let that happen. I live for that. I'm all over the news everyday. I just love it. President Klump looks at his watch. "Excuse me, but I have to go play golf now. When you guys get around to changing White people to Black people, call me, because I want to hang out with some Black dudes since they really know how to have fun. They don't give a shit about anyone or anything except partying. I will pull together a national voting process—it shouldn't take too long."

Rion jumps out of his chair and says, "Wait a minute. What do you mean by Blacks don't care about anyone? I'm Black and I care about my Jewish friends right here in this room."

"We'll all be stuck here on Earth if we don't leave now," whispered Space Girl to her brother, Solar Boy.

President Klump says, "Rion, don't take it the wrong way. I didn't mean that literally. Look, moving on, I'm going to tell NASA to have a chip put on the inside of everyone's right hand. It will contain information about their original race and family origins and history so that in the future we'll know who is really White and who is not. Also, we'll know who's who when we change them back to Black, if we ever do. I mean, sorry, that just slipped out."

Sabrina says, "What difference does it make anyway?"

Reba asks, "But Mr. President, why do you have to know? Can't everyone be the same color—that way things will be equal and fair, at least for awhile."

"Yeah, this way people of color won't

keep getting killed by the Police for no reason," says Rion.

"Now Rion, that's not always the case—the police are just doing their jobs but there are a few exceptions," responded President Klump. "We just have to know who is who, so we can keep tabs on people, as a measure of security. We can't just let everyone come into this country. That's it, that's it! Press Secretary, take a note: To all of Congress, I want a Bill passed for billions of dollars to put up a Wall in outer space. It will be called the "Klump Space Wall" and it will be designed to block certain wormholes from entering our atmosphere, so that bad aliens won't be able to come to Earth, especially to our country, and destroy us."

"But Mr. President," says one of his

advisors, "Can we do that? Don't we need to get the other nations to agree first, and has this ever been done before?"

"Goddamn it, Chauncey, just put billions on it and do it. Let those smart ass scientists earn their money. Now go, get out of here, I need some time to think. Not you Race Changers, I need to know all of your secrets so that our country can get ahead in the race to conquer other Solar Systems. I already have some investments in developing condos and country clubs and golf courses on Mars. I'm also planning to do the same thing on planet Mercury. But don't tell anyone.

"What? Mr. President, don't disclose that information please," says Chauncey.

Sabrina whispers to Rion, "This is

bizarre."

Rion tells Sabrina, "Don't whisper or say anything because we are all on camera being videotaped with microphones everywhere. Tell me later honey."

Reba says, "Mr. President, are you really going to spend billions of dollars to put up walls in space, but not do anything for our environment here on Earth? What's up with that, Sir?" Also, what if you find people on Mars that look like people on Earth, but they are really Aliens, and what if our US astronauts conquer them using violence like they did in the early history of this country? You are already talking about colonizing other planets."

"You know, those are very good questions," responds the President. "I'm sure that NASA has an answer to that somewhere in their secret files, but for now it's top secret information and not for the public. I will announce something on that in the near future. I need to know how your race changing machine works. I think we need to confiscate it for evidence."

Rion says, "I know it's going to be a hard task for you Mr. President, having to go in front of the cameras to the American people about this, especially telling my Black brothers and sisters and my Latino friends and Indian friends that they have to change their color to White."

"No, it will be quite easy. You see, I will go down in history for this decision and most surely get re-elected. The media loves me, see, because I'm a winner, I win at everything I do."

Hours later, after the Race Changers have left the White House, they go to dinner at one of Rion and Sabrina's favorite restaurants—Hogates Seafood Restaurant on the wharf in Southwest DC situated alongside of the Potomac River. But, when they arrive at the restaurant, Rion says, "Damn! They changed the restaurant—it's no longer Hogates. My brother, Bruno told me that there has been many changes made here in DC, but man they used to have the best rum buns, all nice and warm after dinner. It was so much rum in those buns that I almost got pulled over one night for swerving while driving home after dinner.

The Race Changers decided to eat at the new restaurant that was there. They laughed and talked and told stories about their lives. Reba talked about what it was like growing up in South Africa. Then Ava asked Sabrina to tell them what it was like for her growing up in the South.

Sabrina said, "Well, it was fun—for the most part. It wasn't like living in the bigger cities. One day three hippies came to our house in an old beat-up Volkswagen van. It was beat up and had all these crazy designs and wild colors painted on it. There were three guys. One of them had a guitar, one had a banjo, and the third one had a tambourine. They said they were recruiting people to join up with them to go and start a commune in Georgia. They played and sang songs and preached about love and peace. They said they didn't have much money but they plan to grow food on whatever land they settled on. My mother gave them some lemonade but she wouldn't let them in the house. Before they left, they asked for a donation to help fund their purchase for land. My mother gave them a dollar."

Rion says, "Okay, so after hearing that story, I have a question for everyone. Similar scenario, but instead of hippies in the 60s traveling around in old vans recruiting people to put more love and peace in the world, what if good aliens like Solar Boy and Space Girl asked us to go with them to travel to other planets to save good aliens from the hatred of bad aliens? And, in the process, teach love and non-violence. Would you go with them to outer space—to other universes to do good deeds?"

Space Girl started smiling. She asked, "Where is my brother?"

"Yeah, where is he," asked Carlos.

Ava said, "Maybe he went to wash his hands, he disappears at the oddest times."

"Solar Boy has to keep in communication with our parents and top officials of our world. It's hard to explain in English, but he knows what he's doing. We just can't tell you everything about our universe—yet," said Space Girl.

Reba says, "I would love to go with him and Space Girl to be vigilantes in space. What a thrill that would be!"

President Klump is addressing the American people on television. "Everybody, you all have been after my rear end for a while now. So you might as well take your last bite out of it because there won't be anything left to chew on back there after I tell you what I've got to say. I mean—I won't even have a rear end—so when I sit down, I'll be sitting on my back. Get the picture? The people of America are going to have to vote and decide if this country wants to become all White."

"What? What?" whispers a reporter in the press conference. He and another reporter look at each other and start snickering as their camera flashes go off in front of the President.

President Klump takes a drink of water and loosens his necktie. You heard me right—this is the real news. Okay, read my lips. To those of you who are not already a part of the White race, you will have to be changed to White or mankind will be annihilated because of bad aliens who will be here in a few months. When they arrive, if they find any people of color here, Black,

Brown, Yellow or Red, they will destroy planet Earth.

"This is absurd Mr. President, is this some type of experiment?" yells another reporter.

The whole room erupts in cheers, yells, boos and chatter.

Then an African American reporter says, "Maybe this is the best thing that could happen in order to stop so many Black males from being killed by cops all over the US."

"Wait a goddamn minute," says the President. "I want order in here. This is the White House, not church, now listen up." He yells, "I said, get quiet! I will take a few questions now."

TV cameras are rolling in the room with hundreds of reporters.

"How did this prediction of doom come about?" asked a reporter from the Daily News.

"Solar Boy," answered the President. "He is from outer space. I met with him and the Race Changers today in the Oval office."

Another reporter says, "He must be on weed or something, this is bullshit!" Then he walks out of the room.

"Sit down, I'm not finished. Lock the damn doors or I'll have anyone who leaves arrested," the President said angrily.

A White farmer, Dooley Ray, is watching the Press Conference on TV at his home in Southern Virginia. With his heavy Southern drawl, he says to his wife, "Sugar Babe, you ain't gonna believe this. President Klump is gonna have all the people in America to vote on whether all people of color should be changed to White or not."

"Hell naw," says his wife as she walks into the living room from the kitchen. She sits down and starts watching TV with her husband. "He has really lost his ever lovin,' cotton pickin' mind. Who is going to benefit from this stupid shit? Surely not us Whites. What do you think, hun?"

"I'll tell you what I think," says Dooley Ray. "What in the hell is this country coming to? Gosh, darn! I'm going down to the bar in town and meet up with Big Bob and nem. We's gonna talk about this here. My people have always had people of color work for us in the fields and even in the kitchen just helping out. I refuse to let this happen to my family. I'm gonna vote for them not to be changed. I knew this new technology would backfire one day. Can't trust them damn politicians either. If we had enough money I would build a rocket ship and fly our whole family to another planet."

CHAPTER 9 The KKK are At It Again

It's dark outside and it's Halloween night. Solar Boy flies all of the Race Changers to West Hollywood, California. Thousands of people are all dressed up in costumes. It looks like hundreds of them walking on the sidewalks of Hollywood and Vine. People are loud and laughing, shouting and honking their horns. Rion decided to go undercover as an Uber Driver to see what he could find out about Zardoff's devious plan for planet Earth's extinction, and hopefully to find out who he is recruiting. Rion can only inch his way forward with so many people walking in the streets next to the curb, darting in and out of traffic, half tipsy from drinking. It's now 11:00 pm and a call for a pick-up comes in on his cell phone to go to a comedy club on Sunset Boulevard. When he arrives at the club, he sees about 10 White men, about 50-ish standing on the sidewalk in front of the club wearing baseball caps and jeans. When they see the Uber sign on his car, all 10 of them jump in. Rion is driving a small Toyota Corolla.

"What the hell is going on?" Rion shouts.

These guys are literally sitting on each others laps crammed into his small car. It's almost dragging the ground because of the weight of all 10 men.

The leader of the group who is sitting right next to Rion in the front seat says, "Hey boys, look—we got a nigger driving us. Come on, lets get going nigger."

Rion is fuming with anger and mumbles to himself, "What have I gotten myself into here? These fools are drunk." He pulls away from the comedy club. He says to the abusive passenger, "Who are you calling a nigger?"

"You, darky." responded the passenger, "Now drive."

"I can tell you good old boys have been drinking cause your breath is singeing my eyebrows."

"Hey, you almost look like that darky we thought we saw and was about to string up in the desert in Vegas awhile ago. We's the KKK boy, and I am the Grand Dragon. We need some more beers. Take us back to the comedy club. As a matter of fact, why don't you go on stage and tap dance for us like Sammy Davis Jr?"

One of the Klansmen in the back seat says, "Man, we are squished in here like sardines."

Rion says, "You know the police could pull us over for having too many people in this small car. Half of you don't even have seat belts on."

"Just drive boy," said the Grand Master. And that's a small b for boy, but a capital N for nigger. The other Klansmen laugh, their breath smelling like beer, belching and farting, stinking up the whole car.

Rion thinks to himself, *I need to do something to stand up for me and my ancestors, but if I curse them out, they might become violent, then I'll be the one that gets locked up, and they'll go scot-free. So I just have to bite my tongue. I wonder what Martin Luther King would do in a situation like this? I know I won't be able to get any sleep tonight after all of this. I can't wait to tell the Race Changers about it.*

The Grand Master continues, "Why this darky is so bad at driving, he couldn't even drive Miss Daisy." The other Klansman laugh even harder and louder now.

Rion is getting madder and madder. He thinks, *If I was not driving undercover as an Uber Driver, I would take on all of these sons of bitches.*

"Something smells like weed in here. Nigger, have you been smoking weed?"

"No, I haven't," said Rion.

"Cause you've been riding us around for almost an hour and we ain't at our hotel yet."

"You said you wanted to go back to the comedy club. So which is it, your hotel or the comedy club?"

Another Klansman in the back seat says, "I got to go to the bathroom– all of them beers is about to make me explode. Shit! hurry up driver."

The Grand Dragon says, "Hey KKK buddies, I got a great idea. Since it's Halloween night, why don't we go back to our hotel room and put on our White hoods and robes and walk around Beverly Hills and Hollywood, and then we'll go to one of those hotsy totsy mansions and burn a cross in one their front yards. And maybe we'll even go down on Hollywood Blvd and grab a couple of niggers and hang them from one of those big trees in one of them manicured lawns.

They all laugh and slap each other on the back and punch each other in the arm. Another Klansman they call Jim Bob says, "I got another great idea Grand Wizard. We got one darky here right now driving this car." They all stare at Rion with mean looks on their faces.

Rion looks mean right back at them and then pulls out a gun from under his seat and holds it up for them to see and says,

"Don't even try it or I'll make whip cream out of you idiots and put your asses on top of a Coffee Mocha Frappuccino."

Not a word was uttered by any of the 10 Klansmen. They were still blocks from their hotel but all of the men bailed out of the car in a hurry and ran the rest of the way to their hotel room. They changed into their White robes and hoods and walked to Sunset Boulevard and Doheny Street. It was jammed packed with people. Everyone had on costumes. Michael Jackson's song, "Thriller" was blasting from several car radios.

They spotted a young, good looking African American couple. They surrounded them and forced them at gun point to go with them. Two vans pulled up and they all got in and drove a couple of blocks into a residential area of Beverly Hills. They went down a quiet street with no one around and had both people tied up and gagged with their eyes covered. Then a few of them got out of the van and started to burn a cross on one of the manicured lawns. They threw two ropes over two large tree branches and made a noose in both of them and then put them around the necks of the African American couple. By this time, all 10 of the KKK were out of the van standing in the yard. They held torches and said some words as if they were praying to Satan, yelling White Power! Just as they were about to pull the ropes to hoist the two people up and lynch them right there in Beverly Hills on some rich person's lawn, three LAPD police cars came screeching around the corner with their sirens on and Rion leading them in his Toyota Corolla.

The Grand Wizard yelled, "Die Niggers Die."

Surprisingly, out of nowhere appeared

a spaceship in the air above the Klan. It shinned a bright light down on the KKK and made an eerie noise. Then one by one, all 10 of the KKK were lifted up off the ground and were suspended in the air for a few seconds. They all appeared to be frozen in a hypnotic trance. Then a door on the spacecraft opened, and they were all pulled inside of it. The door closed and the mysterious spacecraft took off, disappearing into the night sky.

"Abduction!" yelled one of the Beverly Hills neighbors as she stood in her front yard next door. "I just called the police!"

"Who was that in the spaceship that saved us?" the African American lady asked her partner.

"I don't know, but are you okay, Baby?"

"Yes, I think so." They hugged each other tightly. "I've heard my grandparents talk about lynchings down south hundreds of years ago…I just can't believe what almost happened."

One of the White LAPD officers whispered to his scout car police partner, "Wait a minute, this is Beverly Hills, right? I'm talking mansions, moolah rich-ass White folks, international folks."

His Hispanic fellow police officer said, "Yeah, if there had been a lynching here, it would have been a big story in the newspapers."

Sabrina and the other Race Changers arrive. Solar Boy and Space Girl appear as well. Sabrina runs to Rion and hugs him. She asks, "We need to find out who was in that spaceship that just kidnapped the KKK. Do you know Solar Boy?"

"Well...they are our enemies. They were Zardoff's bad aliens from another galaxy," said Solar Boy.

Far away in deep space, the KKK men are strapped to the wall of the alien spacecraft. They hear Zardoff's voice but cannot see him. He says, "I want to get the hate out of you."

The Grand Dragon says, "You what? You want to knock the shit out of me?" He starts wiggling and jerking trying to break free.

"Calm down you Earth peasant," says Zardoff. "I want to use that hate inside of your brains and clone it or put it in a chip and plant it inside of people, then take them with me when I go to conquer the Universe.

All of space is going to be mine. I am going to spread hate across the entire Universe."

"Are you going to kill us? What are you going to do to us? We're on your side."

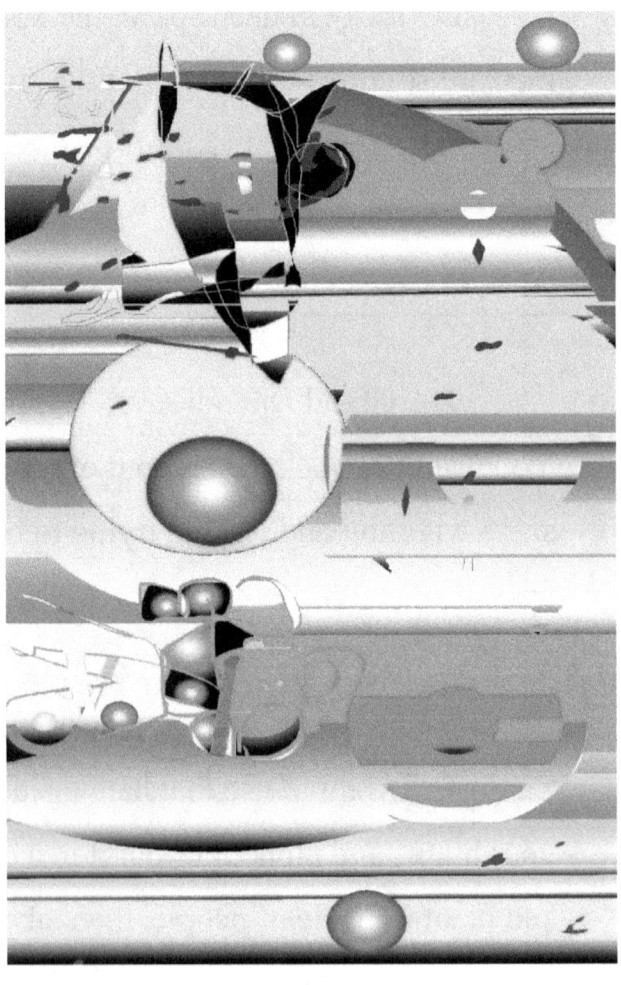

"I am going to operate on your brains."

Meanwhile, back in Beverly Hills, Rion says, "I need a break from all this craziness. Let's go to Sunset Boulevard. Maybe me and Sabrina can get a glass of wine somewhere. Let's go Race Changers."

The Race Changers are now back in the Cadillac SUV. Rion parks it on the street, and they all get out and walk.

"Wow!" says Ava, "Look at all the people here."

Solar Boy says, "This is fun. With my spacesuit on, I blend right in with everyone else wearing costumes. No one is paying any attention to me or Space Girl."

Zoey says, "I wish we had costumes on too."

CHAPTER 10 Bullies: New Alien
Teenage Gang Visits Earth on Halloween

Walking along Sunset Boulevard, Solar Boy says, "I see the Sunbeam Dark Matter gang, all four of them.

Four young guys are dressed in some badass spacesuits and helmets walking slow, looking like the gangsta playas they are.

They are walking towards the Race Changers.

"Who?" asked Rion.

"The Sunbeam Dark Matter gang. They are an alien teenage gang who are also brothers. They are bad beings from another Galaxy. They beat up and rob other kids. I recognize their spacesuits. The tall one is the leader. His name is Sunbeam."

"Here they come," says Reba. "They are walking this way. Look, they are pushing and shoving people out of their way. They just pushed some people into the street. Now they're yelling at them."

"I know," says Solar Boy. "No one gets in their way who knows them. Now one of them is pointing his Laser gun at two people. He just made them disappear."

"What?" says Sharon. They are kind of turning me on."

"Don't even go there," said Reba.

"You know I can get any guy I want, Reba. Anyway, I am really digging those tight pants they are wearing, and damn, look at the bulge on that tall one. I want to go and introduce myself."

Sabrina asks, "Solar Boy, how do you know if they are the Dark Matter aliens?"

Solar Boy answers, "If they took off their helmets, you would see that they are the Dark Matter Aliens."

"In other words, they are Black, right Solar Boy?" asked Rion.

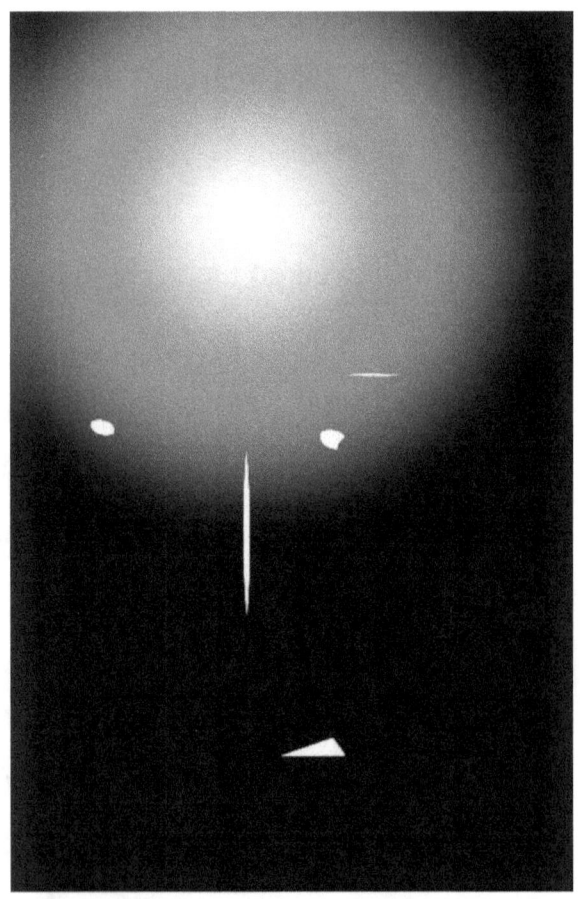

"Yes," responded Solar Boy.

"What are they doing here," asked Reba?

"Not sure, but they are never up to any good. They are my Galaxy's enemies."

"Shouldn't they be in some kind of school somewhere?" asked Rion.

"They dropped out and took to what you all on Earth call 'the streets.' In Galaxy language, they took to 'the hole,' a dark evil place.

"Why are they so mean and evil acting," asked Zoey? "And why are they your enemies? Is it because they are Black and your people are White? My Rabbi said that we should not dislike or hate people who look different from us."

"Zoey is right, so why don't you all get along?" asked Reba.

"That's a very good question Reba," said Solar Boy. "For as long as I can remember it's always been this way in the outer solar systems. It's just a part of existence I guess."

The teenage Alien gang is now right in front of the Race Changers.

"Hey, you punks, give me some money," said the leader, Sunbeam.

"Who in the hell do you think you are talking to," asked Rion. "I'll kick your ass right here and stomp you right into the ground."

Sabrina grabs Rion's arm and pulls him back away from the Dark Matter gang. All of the Race Changers put their hands on their weapons and are ready for battle with serious looks on their faces as though they could kill somebody.

"Hey, I know you," said Sunbeam.

"Yeah, its me, Solar Boy! What are you doing here on Earth, are you following me?"

"No, we're not following you. We are scouting for places that our planet can conquer in this Solar System—not only conquer, but we will easily destroy any civilization that has White inhabitants. You know the Race war in the outer solar systems is getting more fierce and its spreading throughout this Universe which includes Earth. We will be working our way from Pluto towards the sun, planet by planet. My parents and their warriors will be coming here soon. That's all I'm going to say for now."

"What?" says Rion. "I don't believe this. Here we go again—getting into more shit than we can dig our way out of. Now we've got different aliens on our planet at war with each other because they look different. I thought I had seen it all but I guess not. Solar Boy, we need to talk."

"Later, Rion, later."

Sunbeam says, "You're a real space traveler, Solar Boy. You and your galaxy's patrols are one of our enemies. Beware, and be ready."

A gust of wind kicked up just then and all the lights went out in Hollywood. All the people on the streets turned on the flashlights on their cell phones. It provided just enough light for everyone to see, although it was dim, sort of like the light in a nightclub, where people can only see enough to drink and dance, but not be able to tell what anyone really looks like—with all flaws concealed.

"Did you do that?" asked Solar Boy.

"Yeah, I did it, so what?" answered Sunbeam. "What are you going to do about it?" Sunbeam got in Solar Boy's face ready to fight with his hand on his Laser gun.

Solar Boy said, "You better back off and go back to the evil galaxy you slithered out of. Then he pulls his laser rifle out. "I'll send all of you down a Black Hole so far that you'll never see the light of the sun or moon again."

"Damn!" says Rion as he covers his mouth with his hand and then bursts into laughter. "I got it—both of you. Solar Boy, you and the Dark Matter people are from different galaxies and you hate each other, right? Well that's the same thing that's going on right here—on our planet Earth. People of different colors hate each other. I think I've got a solution, at least for now, in this situation."

"Okay honey, spit it out before someone gets killed out here," said Sabrina.

Rion continues, "Okay, let's have a spaceship race between Solar Boy and the Sunbeam gang tomorrow night. We'll have it in Century City near Avenue of the Stars. It's not far from here. They have lots of 30 plus floor skyscrapers. The first one who completes one lap around all of them wins.

So if Solar Boy wins, then both sides will have to become friends, and enemies no more."

Sunbeam and his Dark Matter gang scoffs and becomes irritated. They make sounds that no one has ever heard before. The Race Changers look at each other in disbelief.

"And…if Sunbeam wins," continues Rion, "well, what do you want if you win, Mr. Sunbeam?"

"I want a night alone with this one," replies Sunbeam, looking at Reba. We will have so much fun—if you know what I mean."

Carlos says, "Hey you can't have her, she's my girl."

Then Sunbeam clinches his fist and punches Carlos in the stomach real hard. Carlos has the wind knocked out of him. He bends over holding his stomach.

Reba screams. "Are you okay Carlos?" asked Reba. She puts her arms around him. Looking at Sunbeam, she says, "You didn't have to hit him like that."

Sunbeam laughs and all of his brothers laugh.

"This is a lesson for all of us Race Changers, that when we are around dangerous people, to always have our guard up and be ready to fight," said Rion.

Carlos, now standing up straight again says to the Dark Matter leader, "I am going to get my street gangster Uncle after you."

Then Carlos sees a big piece of metal next to the curb. He picks it up and with a mighty blow hits Sunbeam on the back of his head. He falls to the ground and passes out.

His brothers rush to his side and when he regains consciousness, they help him up. Sunbeam says, "Okay, I'm not finished with you. I'm going to take your girl away because I can. I'll see you all tomorrow night for the skyscraper race in Century City. We will be there waiting for you, so bring your fastest spaceship, and don't forget to bring your girl." Then the Dark Matter gang slinks away like the evil trolls they are.

Solar Boy tells the Race Changers, "I have been in these type of races before and I have the fastest UFO this side of the 27th Galaxy. I will win again.

CHAPTER 11 Bill Diamond's Butler
Spying in Hollywood

About three feet away is Bill Diamond's butler, lurking in the shadows behind a lamppost on the street. He'd been listening all the while to their conversations. Cheap as he is, he wears his Butler's clothes as a Halloween costume and has a black mask on. He's on the phone talking to the corrupt Sherriff in the small town outside of Las Vegas where Bill Diamond lives. He's on a conference call with the Sheriff, the CIA, some Korean Agents and NASA. All of them want the Intergalactic secrets, especially the one of Race Changing with Solar Boy.

"Yeah yeah," the butler says, "I'm here in Hollywood and things are heating up. There's some good looking Persian and

Asian girls out here tonight and they are so drunk, they're actually flirting with me in the clubs and asking me to dance and to go home with them. Just imagine what they would say after they got sober and saw my ugly face drooling all over them."

"Enough! Enough of that foolishness!" says the authoritative voice of the NASA Commander. *"You can get with those chicks later. For now, I want to know what planet Earth can expect in the future."*

"Okay, here goes, believe it or not, there are going to be two invasions here on Earth by two different groups of Aliens. The first will be by Zardoff and his White alien fleet. They will come and destroy mankind if they find any Black people or any other people of color here. After that invasion— get this, the Dark Matter people who are

Black Space Aliens will come to destroy mankind if they find any White people here on Earth."

"Hey everybody, this is the CIA here—that is why we need the Race Changing machine. We need to save at least one race to preserve mankind. NASA, it's up to you smart guys to figure this stuff out."

"I don't like sci-fi stuff, but I am surely going to get paid," says the butler. So uh, just send my $20,000 dollars for this phone call to my bank—just wire it there. I am going to have some fun. Chicks like me! Let's touch base again in a few days. Oh, one thing before I hang up, I really like my boss, Bill Diamond. Please don't tell him that I am a spy."

"You are not just a spy," says the NASA Commander, *"You are very important. You are an Interplanetary Informant."*

"Wow, an Interplanetary Informant," said the butler. "You mean like James Bond—007?"

"No, but you're almost as big. Okay now. I have one question for all of you on this conference call. Do we judge the White aliens as the good guys and help them, or do we judge the Dark Matter aliens as the good guys and help them? Or—he pauses—Do we hate all Aliens that come to Earth because they are different from us, and treat them like the enemy and fend for ourselves?"

"Very good points," said one of the Korean Agents.

"We'll have to ask the President's Space Committee. Let's sign off for now," said the NASA Commander. They all disconnect from the call.

Three gorgeous blonds approach the butler. The tallest one says, "Hey Zorro, you tall, skinny, sexy, hunk of a man, with that dark mask on and wearing those dark clothes—you are turning us Divas on. We are from Sweden. I mean it, you are getting us so hot and sweaty. Lets go to the Love Den night club on Cahuenga so we can have some fun."

"Okay! Your wish is my command, my Tigress!" responds the butler, excitedly.

Then a dark skinned brother walks up with a Jeri Curl and one gold tooth in the front of his mouth tried to come on to the

Swedish girls. The tall Swedish girl says, "Ooh, La La, let's go to the hotel, forget the night club, lets go, my sexy Zorro."

The brother started hailing for a taxi. He said, "I heard you foreign chicks really like the brothers."

When a taxi pulls over to pick them up, the three Swedish girls get in, and then the Butler gets in next to them. But he held the door so that the brother couldn't get in. The brother was trying to force the door open but the butler said, "There's no room for you brother man."

"You better get your damn hand off this door, man, or I'm gonna break your skinny ass in half. And take that damn mask off so I can see whose ass I'll be kicking."

The taxi driver is shouting at all of them to get out of his cab. "I don't want no trouble, ya'll get the hell out of my cab. I need to make some money tonight, and you all are holding me up."

Just then, all the lights came back on in Hollywood. The girls take a good look at the butler and at the Black guy. The tall Swedish girl says, "Let's go Zorro and leave this countryfied farm boy with his greasy ass Jeri curl behind. I thought Jeri curls went out of style in the 80s."

"Wait a minute," says the brother. What happened to your accent? You ain't Swedish! You might be Ho-ish, but you show ain't Swedish! Where are you from, Texas or North Kakalakie? I can hear a southern accent in your voice now. And you, Mr. Zorro, you show ain't gonna have all

three of these fake blond chicks to yourself."
He finally gets the cab door free and forces
his way into the cab and sits on the Butler's
lap. The Butler pushes him off and all five
of them are crammed into the back seat of
the cab twisted up like pretzels.

"Damn! he got some Jeri curl juice on
my leopard skin dress," said one of the girls.

"See," says the butler. "They don't
want you." The cab finally pulls off.

"Shut up you freak, says the brother,
and take that mask off." You don't know
shit. I know I can show them a good time.
What can you do for them except show them
which way is the closest old folks home. I
bet you're a wrinkled up old man behind
that mask."

The third quiet girl takes out a bottle of vodka from her purse and takes a couple of sips. "Damn," says the brother, "Somebody is going to get their freak on tonight!" Then he laughs and rubs his hands together. "Yes indeed."

CHAPTER 12 Spaceships Race in
Century City

It's midnight in Century City. There

are two sleek, shiny spaceships with bright

lights hovering next to the Hilton Hotel skyscraper of about 40 floors.

"Okay, this is the starting point and the finish line," said Solar Boy, speaking into the microphone of his headset, while sitting in the cockpit of his spacecraft. "The first one to circle every building in this block wins. There are 10 buildings. Ready, set, go!"

They both take off with Solar Boy taking the lead, but the Dark Matter bullies are not far behind. They whiz around and between buildings and are flying so fast that it shatters the windows in some of the buildings. People on the ground are looking up at the race. Some people are calling the police and others call some radio and TV stations complaining of UFO's racing at high speeds. The Air Force is called out.

They are interfering with the race, trying to distract the two spaceships. Reba is aboard Solar Boy's spaceship.

"I am in the lead but I can't go on—I am about to pass out, can you help me Reba?" asked Solar Boy.

"What?" Reba screams.

"Sometimes if I go months without eating, I get a condition that your people refer to as 'Vertigo.'

"Who on Earth goes months without eating?"

"I'm not from Earth Reba, remember?"

"Please, no!" pleads Reba. "I don't know how to fly this thing!"

"When I'm flying alone and get Vertigo, all I have to do is flip the spaceship and fly it upside down. For whatever reason, it works."

"Then do it now," asked Reba, "Do it now!"

"I can't because you're in here with me and you would surely get sick if I did that. So, take the controls on your side, and I'll tell you what to do—I'll try not to pass out."

"Pass out? What the hell, Solar Boy. I'll probably pass out from fear so we'll both be goners."

"Just listen to me Reba, I'm fading. You don't have to touch any controls. The ship can be powered by your thoughts. Just think about where you want the ship to go and it will follow your thoughts and take you there, but you have to stay focused." Solar Boy then passes out.

"Oh, shiiiiiit! Here I go….think, think, think," said Reba, talking to herself. "Where do I want this spaceship to go? I have to dodge birds, helicopters, planes and all kinds of stuff. Well, I'll just keep trying because Miss Sabrina said to do something great, so here I go."

After about 15 minutes the race is finished and the two spacecraft land in an open field. Solar Boy wins the race! No one will ever know that it was Reba who actually won the race, if they don't tell anyone. When Solar Boy regains consciousness, he and Reba get out of their spacecraft and approach the Dark Matter gang. Sunbeam shakes Solar Boy's hand and says, "Let's work together. Even though we look different— we are Black aliens and you are White aliens, maybe we can stop the invasions that are about to happen to Earth."

"Great! We're Allies now," responded Solar Boy.

Reba says, "Sunbeam, there's a Homecoming dance after the football game Friday night at my school. Would you and your brothers like to come?"

"That's a good idea," said Solar Boy. "I hear that there might be some trouble with some bad aliens looking for me. You all can be my back up. How about it Dark Matter people, will you come to her school?"

But you can't wear what you have on now, you'll stand out too much. People will start asking questions," said Reba.

"We will do a transformation so that we look more like your brown friend, Rion. But yes, we will come—what is the location?"

"Alabasas High, at 7 pm on Friday," said Reba.

"Okay, see you there."

It's now Friday night and Alabasas High football team is playing Brenshaw High at the Alabasas school field in the Valley. The game is close and Alabasas football team wins by one point in the last few seconds. Later that night, everyone was excited and arriving at the Homecoming dance. Solar Boy, Space Girl, the Race Changers and the Dark Matter alien gang are there.

The DJ was playing music and people were dancing and having a good time. After a couple of hours, one of the star football players, a White guy named Joey is standing outside of the gym talking to some friends. Suddenly, out of nowhere, three hoopty cars with tinted windows speed up together and race towards Joey. He pays it no mind and just continues to talk to his friends. Then the window rolls down and a Black kid with long braids and a bandana wrapped around his head shouts, "There's the dude who made the touchdown and made us lose the game! Let's cap that son of a bitch. Lock and load—let's get him homies." Then, as Joey walks away from his friends, two Black guys and one Spanish kid jump out of their cars and run real fast, half way up the walkway to the gym and opens fire on Joey. Shots rang out in the night air, as well as screams from the kids nearby. Joey falls to the ground with his green and gold letterman's jacket all bloody.

"Duck, run, run!" screamed several people. Some students hit the ground to protect themselves, others ran. Three hoodlum shooters jump in their cars and speed away, burning rubber and screeching tires that could be heard blocks away. Lots more students run out of the gym to see what was going on, including the Race Changers.

"Solar Boy, come quick," yells Reba. ,Look—look what they did to Joey. All of the Race Changers gather around him. He's unconscious and his eyes are closed. "Why did they do this?"

One of the teachers gives him first aid and then another teacher yells, "Call 911 and tell them to send an ambulance."

Solar Boy was standing alongside the Black Matter alien teens. He asked, "Who did this?"

Reba answered, "I was outside and I heard one of them say something like, 'This is for Brenshaw High—since you won the game, we are going to cap your ass.' "

"What did the car and the shooters look like, asked Space Girl?"

Zoey described the cars and the
shooters.

"Come on Race Changers, we're
going after them," said Solar Boy.

The Dark Matter teen leader says,
"We're going to follow you. We'll help you
get those bad guys."

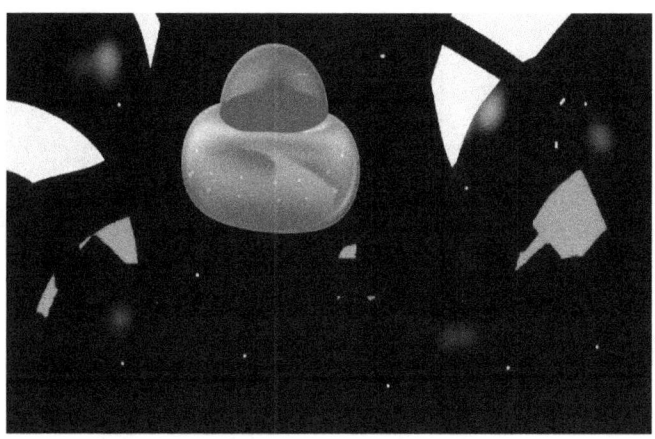

Both alien groups jump in their
spaceships, and from above they were able
to locate the cars speeding down the 405
freeway.

Zoey asks, "Why would they want to shoot Joey? Is it because he was White? If he was a Black guy, would they still have shot him?"

Rion answers, "Yes, those types from the streets, they don't care. They will rob and steal from their own mother. There can be people like that in any race."

"I hope he makes it," said Reba. "We had some classes together. We were friends. I was so scarred hearing those gunshots, and it happened so fast."

Solar Boy spots the culprits from his spaceship.

"Look, there they are," said Solar Boy.

They are all at the Watts Towers now. The LAPD are now behind the shooters' cars. They start shooting at them. The hoodlums jump out of their cars and run. They jump over a fence into someone's yard. Both spaceships land and one of the Dark Matter guys run after the hoodlums. When he gets ready to jump the fence in pursuit of them, a White Los Angeles police officer yells, "Stop or I'll shoot." But the officer immediately shoots five times and all five shots hit the Black Matter teen in the back and he dies on the spot.

Rion says, "Damn! They killed one of the Dark Matter Aliens." Then there is an eerie silence. The wind stops blowing and the cars stop moving. The remaining three Dark Matter aliens float in formation out of their spaceship. They lift up their deceased brother's body over their heads, and then float back up into their spaceship. They took over the media radio and TV stations and gave a warning saying, "We are the Dark Matter Aliens and our father is King of our Solar System. He will be come back for revenge for the killing of his son. He will bring with him a fleet of aliens so big that their ships will fill up your entire atmosphere. It will take us one year to return from the outer Galaxy, billions of light years away. This was always our Plan, but when we made peace with Solar Boy, we changed it. Now you have killed one of ours, so our original Plan is back in effect, and that is— to destroy Earth when we return if we find any White people here."

CHAPTER 13 Reba's Science Project

A few days later, Reba wants to return to her school to see her classmates.

"Are you sure you want to go back to your school right now Reba with everything that's been happening?" asked Sabrina.

"Yes, yes, I'm sure....I love the life of a Race Changer. I just need to feel normal again and be around my school friends and see how they're doing. The only person I'm nervous about seeing is Roxanne. She told me that if I didn't bring her $10,000 dollars, she's going to kill my cat and dog. She's a real bitch too. Nobody likes her except some of the other gangster girls from Simi Valley. All they wear is those plaid long sleeve shirts and beany caps. They carry straight razors and knives and they will cut you in a minute."

Sabrina looks at Rion. "Alright Reba," said Rion. We'll let you return there, but only for a few hours. You must watch your back at all times. Take Zoey with you. Sabrina and I are responsible for both of you, and your parents are counting on us to keep you safe."

So Reba and Zoey go back to Alabasas High School. They drop in on Reba's Science class. She's greeted by some of her girlfriends. They have seen her on TV. One of them asks her, "How does it feel to be a famous living pioneer of the Alien Revolution, Reba?"

"It's okay, but it's tiring," said Reba.

The teacher sees them. "Well, well, well," says Mr. Deverkill. "Class, look who decided to pay us a visit. It's that new scientific world-saving superstar Reba, and her sister." Some of the class applauds and cheers and some of them boo. "We have not seen you all semester. I hope you brought your final Science project with you."

"Uh, Science project?" asked Reba.

"Yes, you have to do something that will make me not fail you because of all the days you've missed class."

In the meantime, Zoey is on her phone with Solar Boy. She tells him the position that Reba is in, and that she needs to turn in a Science project.

"Don't worry," says Solar Boy. "Just be ready to run out of class in a few minutes. Something crazy is going to happen."

Zoey goes over to Reba and whispers in her ear.

I have my Science project!" Mr. Deverkill," Reba shouts with excitement.

"Well, let's see it," said Mr. Deverkill.

Reba addresses the class. "Okay, class, turn off the lights in the room and turn off your cell phones too, and then close your eyes." So the class did what she requested. "I am going to clap my hands three times, and after I do, you can open your eyes."

She claps her hands three times, and the

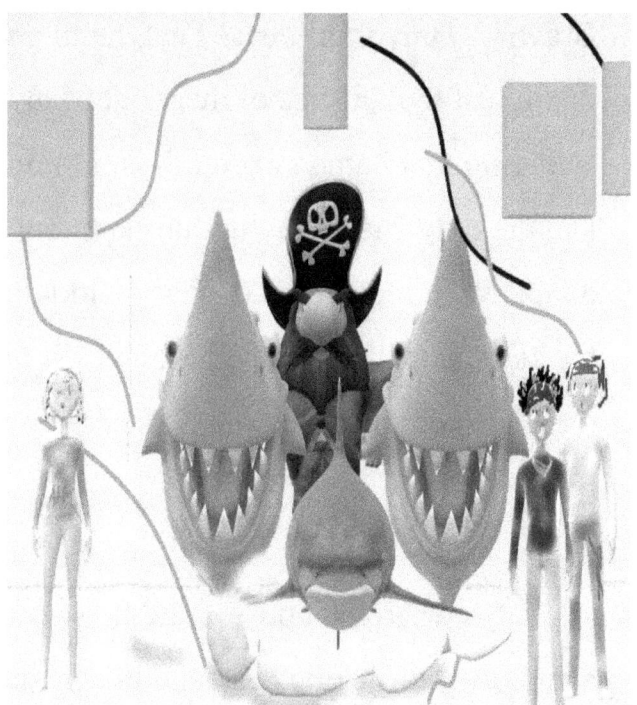

students open their eyes. Through the wall in the
front of the class where the clock was hanging
came a large scary looking ghost pirate swinging a
sword. He kept flashing in and out, visible and
then invisible. The students all scream and the
teacher who is already weird and very nerdy
looking, stands on top of his desk. His eyeglasses
are foggy. He applauds and yells "Bravo! Bravo!
Bravo! You get an A plus! Reba."

A Black student said, "Bravo?—
Bravo?—Bravo for what? That damn ghost
pirate just took a slice of meat out of my leg,
swinging that damn sword of his. I know
I'm the only Black guy in this class, but
damn! Why me! Come on Gary—looking at
his classmate, "Grab that desk and I'll pick
up this chair and we'll knock the crap out of
him."

So when the ghost pirate flies by them
again, they throw the desk and the chair at
him. It doesn't even phase the ghost pirate in
the least because both objects went right
through him. By now, a trail of blood is on
the floor from the student's leg.

"I'm going to kick this dude's ass,"
says the Black guy.

The class kept screaming, knocking over tables, chairs and books, ducking and running from the ghost pirate. He kept swinging his sword, trying to chop off about 30 students' heads. The students ran out of the classroom and out of the school. Reba and Zoey also ran out of the school to safety. Zoey was laughing with Reba and told her that Solar Boy just opened up a wormhole and that's how the ghost pirate appeared.

Reba said, "Well at least I got an A+ for my grade and only went to class one day out of the semester."

After Reba and Zoey ran out of the classroom, they looked back and saw the pirate ghost chasing kids, waving his sword yelling at them, "I'm going to chop your heads off." In the hallway, the Science teacher is standing with his arms folded looking mad. He yells to the kids who are freaking out, knocking each other down trying to escape, "See what can happen to you if you don't come to class prepared?"

Reba says to Zoey, "OMG, here comes Adrian, Captain of the basketball team. Remember, I used to date him for awhile. Damn! My hair is a mess—oh, he's so cute! Zoey, tell the others I'll catch up with them later."

"Okay, but don't be long or you know Mr. Rion and Ms. Sabrina will be looking for you." Then Zoey walked back into the school.

Adrian approaches Reba with some of his cronies and says, "Hey Hotty! You know you and your sister are stars now cause you're Race Changers. All the girls are jealous of you too. Everywhere you go there's trouble with aliens. I'd love to join up with your group. I got mad skills. I'd be as asset to your group." Then he takes a swig out of a can of beer he has concealed in a paper bag.

"Well, I'll have to see," says Reba. Lots of kids have been asking to join up with us. But, for sure, I'll put in a good word for you." Reba bats her eye lashes and blushes.

Adrian says, "Me and some of the other basketball players were hanging out in the cemetery in Culver City last Friday night, drinking beer. And we heard some zombies talking. They said they were going to turn some Gangster Ghosts loose so they could capture you, and then kill you and take you back to the underground world with them.

Reba laughs, "Really? What are Gangster Ghosts?"

"They are dead people who used to be thug gangsters. They are meaner that just plain ghosts. These dead dudes will just fly through you and suck the life right out of you on the spot. You can always tell a Gangster Ghost because they always wear a hat tipped to one side, and when they are flying in the air, they don't fly straight, they fly with a gangster lean. They are the worst ghosts there is, and you don't want to mess with them. They will jump you and take you out. They can even become invisible and if you don't keep thinking positive, they can cause things to go wrong in your life. Ever since the invasion started, the bad aliens have connected with the ghosts of those that have been killed by their lovers. They have also been programmed to come after special people like you because they want to bump up their population." He hands Reba his beer and says, "Here, chug-a-lug."

Reba hesitates and says, "Uh, I don't like beer, I'd rather not."

"Oh, I see," says Adrian, "You're innocent, like a little baby."

She then grabs his beer and takes a long swig out of it, then hands it back to him. "Don't ever call me a baby, you asshole. I've already killed ghosts and zombies and bad aliens with my laser weapon. So you don't know me very well."

She starts to walk away from him, but he grabs her and kisses her on the lips. She did not expect that. Her face turns red and she tries to walk away again, but this time he grabs her and presses his body up against hers and says, "When you turn red. I know what that means, baby. It means that you want me. You forgot that I am Captain of the Basketball team and the redder you get, the more it turns me on." He kisses her again, but this time she does not resist. His buddies hoop and holler with excitement. "Come on baby, let's go to that vacant house across the street from the school and have some fun."

"I have a boyfriend, and his name is Carlos."

"So what? I'll screw you and Carlos too if he gets in my way. Now come on

Baby cause I'm packin' and I don't mean with a weapon either."

He puts his arm around her waist and they walk off the school property and across the street to the vacant house. He uses his credit card to trip the lock of the back door. They both turn their cell phones off. They spend the night there and the next day they go to school together.

While in class, Reba calls her sister. *"Where on Earth are you, Reba? We've all been worried sick about you. And you know we couldn't risk calling the cops."* says Zoey.

Reba whispers into the phone, "I'm in class right now."

"Where were you yesterday and last night?"

"I did a bad thing Zoey, and I feel ashamed. I just had to get away from all the pressure." While talking to Zoey, Reba texts some of her friends and sends them a photo of her and Adrian hugging, naked from the waist up.

Zoey asks, *"What do you mean you did a bad thing?"*

"I made love to Adrian. I might still be in love with him. We really made out last night. But right now, I feel terrible because I cheated on Carlos. I have his friendship ring and we are supposed to get married in a few years. Look, Zoey, whatever you do, don't tell Mom and Dad. They would kill me.

They like Carlos. What do I do, Sis? I'm so confused."

"Reba, I know you're still a virgin, girl. Don't try to fool me—you made a chastity vow three years ago that you would not have sex until you were 18."

"Well, I almost did. I took my blouse off and we hugged and kissed all night, and if you ever tell anyone that we didn't make love, I'll never speak to you again. I like being popular, but being a virgin doesn't equal popular."

"Okay, Sis, it'll be our little secret. But tell me something, how did you keep Adrian from just taking it from you? He can be a bit of a bully sometimes. He thinks he's God's gift to girls."

"That's for me to know and you to find out, Zoey."

"Yeah, okay Reba....I'll get it out of you sooner or later."

CHAPTER 14 America's Votes!

It is now November, and very soon it will be the Presidential Election day, and on the ballot is a question of whether to change all people of color to White to save the planet.

"I don't believe I'm hearing this," said Rion. You mean to tell me that the President is really going to let the people vote on changing all people of color to White? And then take a chance on getting re-elected for four more years?"

"Yep," says Sabrina. "I have never heard of anything like that in my whole life. I heard that last Sunday, at our church, the Pastor talked about it in his sermon. You know our church members are predominantly Black. Well, he asked how many people in the congregation would be willing to be changed into White people to save our planet? He asked them to raise their hands if they would do it, and every person of color raised their hands. He said that the Solar System is going through changes right now and that they had better get on board and learn how to deal with new situations."

"You know what?" asked Reba, "I heard that my Rabbi asked the opposite question last Saturday at our Shabbat service. He said, "By a show of hands, how many of you would be willing to change into a Black person if it meant saving our planet?' Only three people out of all 300 raised their hands."

Rion said, "Is this something that Martin Luther King would have wanted for America? Would he tell them to change to

White if they were Black? Or to change to Black if they were White, in order to save planet Earth?"

Sharon asked, "Would the Rabbi still be Jewish if the color of his skin changed?"

"Yes," said Ava. "Rabbi said Jews come in all colors. And that they are not White, they are Jewish."

After the election, President Klump goes on national TV and Twitter is set on fire after he announces to the American people that the majority of Americans voted for people of color to be changed to White by January 1st. He also said for all of those who are willing to be changed without resisting, they will receive an additional one half of their monthly salary for six months.

Rion said, "See—immediate benefits of being White." All the Race Changers laugh.

"You want to hear something funny?" asked Rion. "I was talking on the phone to one of my best friends in DC the other day, and he told me that some Black dude in the hood were building and selling spaceships that can space travel to another planet for only $500.00." All of the Race Changers laugh.

"I heard of this guy too," said Carlos. "He's walking around in some type of space-looking suit with a football helmet on, telling people to follow him into the alley where he has his space missile on a launching pad.

"That's a lie," Rion said, "That guy is all fake. My boy in DC told me that he just lures people into the alley with a fraudulent story, and out-slicks them and their families for money. Then after he gets them deep into the alley, away from other people, he and his partners pull their guns out and rob them. People can be so gullible, but nowadays, anything is possible. You know this type of scamming goes on all day, every day in the hood."

"Yeah, tell us Jewish American Princesses one more story about the hood, Mr. Rion, so we will know how to survive," asked Ava.

"Later Ava—now lets get on with our mission."

CHAPTER 15 Race Changing in America, Dealing With the Chaos

"Solar boy, there is only one month left, Solar Boy, before Zardoff comes to invade Earth and maybe destroy it," says Reba. "What are we going to do, we don't even have one eighth of the planet changed to White."

Ava says, "I have another question. Will the people that were born White on Earth think that they are better than the people that were changed to White?"

"Good question," says Sabrina. "What I want to know is how will the original White people be able to tell who the newly-changed White people are?"

Rion says, "Well now, from my experience with people, the original Whites will judge people that are newly Whites a little different. They will probably say that they are better than the others. But who cares, we are just trying to survive two invasions."

"Two invasions?" asked Carlos.

"Yes, the news reports are saying that word is out about people's skin color being changed to Black because of the impending Dark Matter alien invasion. Some rich Whites are vehemently making plans to travel to other planets so they won't have to be changed into Black people. They say that for some Whites, it would be worst than the stock market crash of 1929."

"That is totally ludicrous," says Sabrina.

Reba said, "I bet that most of them are old fashioned people too, cause even the kids in my class at school know that it's really dope to hang out with Black kids."

"I agree," said Sharon. "Of course, they will find only White people here because our whole planet will be White, unless something goes wrong and Zardoff destroys Earth—which I can't bear to think about."

"Don't say that too loud," says Sabrina, "cause you know Zardoff can read peoples' minds and we don't want to draw him here."

"Okay, enough philosophizing on what could happen, should happen, or ought to happen," said Rion. Solar Boy, how do we change every person of color on Earth to White by January 1st? I don't want to wake up and have my head on a serving tray in front of some King of the Aliens ready to be eaten?"

Solar Boy whispers something to Space Girl and then they both high five each other. Solar boy says, "This is what we're going to do. We can easily make millions of our Race Changing laser guns that will only work until January 1st, then after that, they will disappear. I will have our Robot spaceships drop them off at Police stations, Military bases, and Airports in every country. I will hold a press conference and tell the world how to use them. If everyone cooperates, this will work and we can save planet Earth.

"That is a brilliant idea!" exclaimed Reba.

"Okay, I will get right on that."

"Look at this," says Sharon, as she turns her cell phone around for everyone to see. The evening news is on her phone reporting that some rednecks in a small town bar in Georgia are shooting their guns in the air yelling and cursing. One of them shouted, "Put our General Robert E. Lee statue back up in the town square and put our ancestors' Confederate flag up!" Then they all cheered and yelled "White Power! White Power! White Power!"

People are going crazy all over the world. Some people of color are killed by White rebels, retaliating. But many Blacks and people of color fight back in self-defense. Some of Rion's friends from Jr. High School who had become millionaires in Washington, DC called and told him that they were proud of what he was doing. They said they were ready for a fight, and that they had their guns and ammo ready for when the Aliens come. These guys were some of the meanest dudes from the toughest neighborhoods in DC where Rion grew up. Their motto was, 'We run from nothing, but if we run, we run *to* a fight, not *from* a fight.'

Some Black families were shown on TV news leaving the big cities and going to the country to hide out in mountains and caves. Black preachers and Rabbis had always told their congregations to do what law enforcement and the President says because it was the right thing to do. But this time they told them, 'You must make your own decision.'

The Race Changers go to Mexico to check on Carlos' grandparents. While sitting with his grandparents on their front porch, his 95 year old grandfather says, "I am going to sit right here on this front porch with my 93 year old wife, and I am not going to let them change her. I am going to wait on the good Lord to take her, not some strange aliens from space."

"I agree," said Carlos. "Besides, they have to get pass those badass bandidos here in Mexico first, and you know they will kill anybody. I think the bandidos will team up with the Mexican Police and fight the aliens to save themselves and their way of life.

One of Carlos' cousins is sitting in his grandparents back courtyard with some tough guys drinking tequila and watching roosters fight. They have a small TV outside with a twisted coat hanger wired to it for an antenna. They are listening to the news and all the crazy events going on all around the world. His cousin yells, "Aliens? I ain't afraid of no goddamn Aliens! Come on down here. I got something for you." Then he shoots several rounds off with his AK 47 rifle at some trees and into the air.

Meanwhile, on the front porch Carlos' grandfather says, "Nobody in our Spanish community is going to want to be changed, Carlos."

"I know Grandpa, I know. But if you don't let us change you, the Mexican government will. We all have to try and save the world, Grandpa."

Tears form in his grandmother's eyes. Carlos goes over and hugs her. The Race Changer girls and Sabrina have tears in their eyes too.

Rion tells the group that he heard the President declared the month of November as Space month and since it's also the Election month, and less than two months before the invasion in January, he said he will make the stock market go through the roof and turn the 1% of American billionaires into trillionaires. He said if the planet doesn't make it, then at least some people will have a good time and die richer on their way out.

Rion's cell phone rings and he answers it.

"Hello."

"Hey Rion, it's me."

"Is this wild Bill?" asked Rion.

"You bet your bank account it's me, better yet, my fat bank account. Man, have I got a scoop for you. Where is your Race Changer group right now?"

"We're in Mexico visiting Carlos' grandparents."

"My friend, here's the deal. I just got through talking to my maid's son on the phone. You know he's been on the run because he discovered some secrets about

Area 52 when he was working there. He said for you guys to be careful because the powers that be or Big Brother is experimenting with this hate thing. He's going to try to make it here to my ranch and tell us what he found out while he was held captive at Area 52. I think you Race Changers should be here at the same time. It could be crucial to your mission. He will be here in a few days.

"You know, you're right Bill. Your place will be our next stop. When Luce's brother arrives, don't let him leave. We want to see him and hear what he has to say."

"Okay, partner. Be safe and don't look anyone in the eye. You never know who they might be. They could be aliens or zombies trying to take your soul. At this point, you can't trust anyone. Looking

forward to seeing my nieces again. Thanks
my man for keeping them safe. I'll have my
cook fix you all some good ribeye steaks and
your favorite potato salad, Rion"

"Okay, Bill, see you soon."

CHAPTER 16 Supernatural Lightening
Strikes on Bill Diamond's Ranch

The Race Changers arrive at Bill
Diamond's ranch. They exchange hugs and
greetings with Bill's maid, Luce. They all go
into the dining room. The table is set
beautifully for them.

Rion asks Luce, "Where is Bill?"

Right then, Bill Diamond yells in a
child-like voice, "I'm out here!"

The Race Changers run into the grand
foyer just in time to see Wild Bill with his
signature white cowboy hat and white boots
on jump from the second floor balcony onto
the chandelier and swing back and forth.
Then he lets go of it and lands below on the
first floor right next to the Race Changers.

"Great entrance, Bill!" says Rion. They all applaud.

Grinning from ear to ear as if he'd been expecting the applause, Bill hugs his nieces and everyone else, now that they are all kind of like family.

"So where is he, Bill?"

"Where is who?" asked Bill.

"Your maid's son."

"Oh, yes, yes, right. Looking at Luce, Bill says, "Have Claude join us for dinner. He can tell us all at one time about his experience at Area 52."

"Mr. Diamond, I'm not sure he's up to seeing anyone right now," says Luce.

"Well, he'd better be up for it. These guys need all the information they can squeeze out of him cause Doomsday could be just around the corner. Now go fetch him woman."

"Yes, sir."

"Sit down everybody," says Bill. Don't be shy now.

They all sit down at the table and take a sip of their beverages. In walks Claude, Luce's son. His thin, straight black hair is plastered to his head and his eyeballs are bulging. He doesn't even blink. He's wearing a gray beanie and his black hair is sticking out of the sides and back of it. His nose is pointed and hooked like a bird's beak. His tall, thin frame and scraggly goatee makes him look like a hippie from back in the 60s. His blank stare gives the impression that he could have been heavily drugged while at Area 52. He's only 30 years old, but he looks 50. It's hard to tell. He sits down at the table and starts looking around as if something is going to jump out at him any second. The Race Changers are becoming nervous just looking at him. Sabrina leans over to Rion and asks, "What in the hell, Rion? What is wrong with him? I'm getting dizzy just looking at him."

Rion pats Sabrina on the hand and says, "It's okay honey, he's been through a lot."

You could hear a pin drop. Everyone is so quiet, including Bill Diamond. All of a sudden, Claude jumps up from the table. He scared everybody. Then he says, "I thought it was them. I thought I heard something. I hear them thinking. They are plotting to kill me!" He walks over and opens the door to an adjacent room, then closes it. His mother, Luce leads him back to the table. He sits back down.

Bill downs his brandy in one gulp. He holds his glass up and says, "Another one, Luce."

Luce goes over and takes his glass, then walks over to the wet bar, refills it and brings it back to him. The room is silent.

Rion says, "Claude, we do understand that you've had a traumatic experience when you were held captive at Area 52. And believe me, if this wasn't a matter of life and death, we wouldn't make you relive it again by talking about it. But for the sake of all humanity on planet Earth, do you think you could bear to tell us what happened there? More importantly, what is the evil enemy planning?"

Reba whispers to Ava, "Is he a robot or is he a human?"

Claude heard Reba and said, "I'm not sure. I am still human as far as I know. I was a janitor at Area 52. I worked the midnight shift."

Rion says, "For now, don't anyone interrupt. Lets just listen to what Claude has to say."

Claude tells his story. "On the way to work one night, my car stopped right after I saw a flash of lightning. Then I saw six UFOs in the sky. They were some kind of little circular aircrafts that kept moving back and forth. Then they disappeared over a mountain close to work. After I saw that, I couldn't get my car to start. A few minutes later two blue vans with dark tinted windows drove up and blocked the road in front of me. Three men got out. They were wearing white spacesuits and had helmets on. I was really scared and reached for my gun, but before I could use it, they took it from me.

They pulled me out of the car. One of them stuck a needle in my arm. I remember seeing Area 52 on the front of their helmets. They dragged me over to their van and put me in it. I asked them where they were taking me? I told them that I wanted to talk to the person in charge. Then I must have went unconscious because the next thing I remember was raising my head up and gazing out of the van's window. I saw a sign that said Area 52 U.S. Government Keep Out.

I passed out again and when I came to, I found myself looking up into a bright light inside of a huge laboratory. Then I realized that the bright light was some type

of mini UFO hovercraft in the air about 10 feet above me. I was strapped down on a table wearing nothing but a hospital gown. There were about six people with surgical masks and lab coats on holding needles and tubes. On a table next to me in jars were some type of snakes, a black crow and some butterflies. There were hoses attached connecting them all together. Then one of them inserted a needle into an IV that was in my arm and injected something into it. Then they implanted some type of chip in the back of my neck. I could see all this going on, but I felt no pain. I heard them talking about some kind of colonization in outer space with hate robots that are half-human and half-alien. They said they were doing this to experiment to make it so that I could live in outer space without oxygen and spread hate.

Then the hovercraft that was above me started to shake and twirl around. It twirled all around the room. Then it crashed into the wall.

Alarms started going off. One of the scientists yelled, 'Run, run for your life.' Then, one of the walls raised up and some type of aliens came in walking towards me. I said to myself, *Holly shit, I better get my Italian ass out of here.* Then there was an explosion and a fire broke out and there were even more alarms going off. I don't know how, but I was able to break loose from the straps that held me down. I jumped off the table and started running for the door. I don't know where the Scientists went because the door was still locked. There must have been a secret exit door somewhere. It must have been my lucky day because I found a keycard on the floor that one of the Scientists must have dropped, so I used it to open the door. I ran out with several alien creatures chasing me. I was running from lab to lab through warehouses and dark corridors. I saw all kinds of UFOs and alien creatures that scared the hell out of me. I saw robots and cameras in security rooms. I hid in one of them for a few minutes.

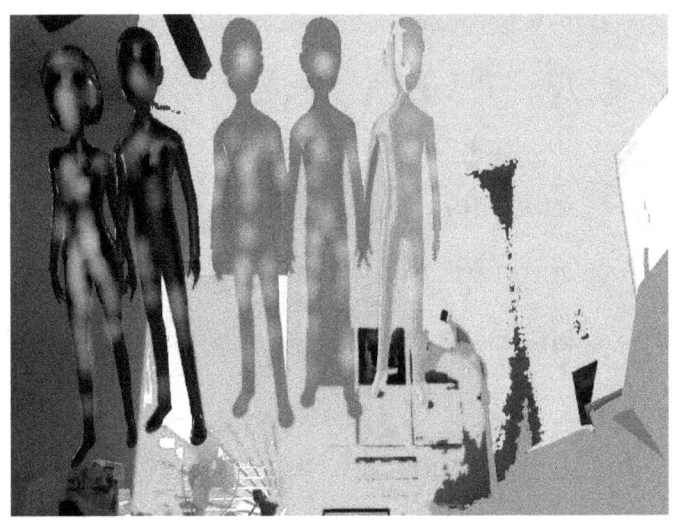

There were maps of several countries on the walls and what looked like other planets, I guess. It was clear to me somehow that they were out to conquer the people that occupied them. I pulled out my camera and took photos and grabbed some top secret folders and ran outside. I jumped in a van that still had the key in the ignition. There were several Army patrol security men who saw me escaping and speeding off. They ran towards me and began shooting at me with their rifles. I heard a voice yell, 'Kill him, kill him, he has some of our secret plans. He must not get away.' I floored the gas petal in the van and I was almost out of there, but suddenly the van stopped right before I could get to the main gate. Man, I was almost free.

I looked to my left and saw a beautiful woman sitting in a small hovercraft smiling at me. She waived to me to come and go with her. I don't know why but I trusted her. So I jumped out of the van and got into her hovercraft. She said, 'I will fly us over the compound wall and down the mountain out of Area 52 and you can stay at my place.' We flew straight up in the air over the wall with bullets flying behind us."

A silence fell over the room.
Everyone at Bill Diamond's dinner table
was trying to process what Claude had just
told them. Then for no apparent reason,
Claude started to laugh in a loud, deep

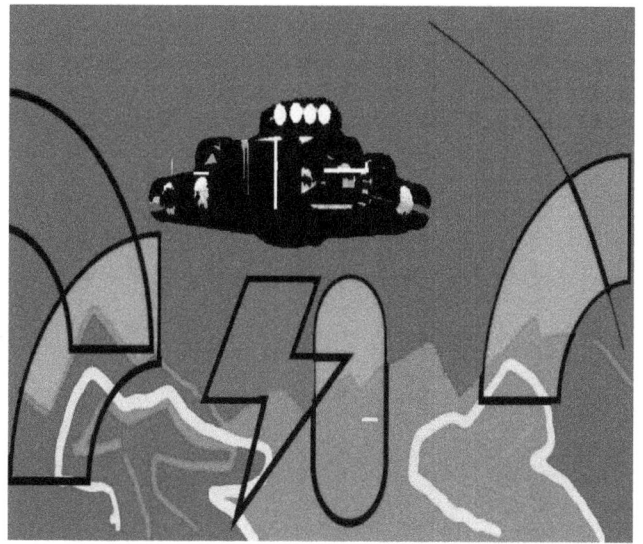

voice. Reba said, "I'm scared." Then there
was a very loud clap of thunder. The wind
began to kick up and whistle outside, and
the lights went out all over the house. It was
pitch-black. Lightening came in through one
window, moved around the room creating
images of everyone's shadows on the walls.

It was both frightening and mystical as the lightening found its way back out through another window.

"Sweetheart, Sweetheart!" yelled Sabrina. "Where are you? Its dark in here, I can't see."

Bill Diamond yells, "Don't be afraid, I have some candles here, somewhere, just hold on. And while I'm at it, I'll pull out my automatic SAR 80 rifle."

"I'm over here," Rion yells.

Thunder is crashing above the mansion. When Bill gets the candles lit, Luce screams, "Where is my son? He's gone! He knows too much secret information."

Then Zoey screams, "Where is my sister?"

The lights suddenly come back on. The thundering and lightening stopped.

Bill Diamond says, "And Reba is leading a mission to save the world, and she disappeared too. Where could they have gone?" He loads his gun. "Don't worry guys, we'll find them. If I have to take out ghosts or vampires or any enemy forces, believe me, we will find them."

To be continued in Volume III...